Alpha's Claim

Bad Boy Bears
Book 1

Renee Rose

Lee Savino

Midnight
ROMANCE

Want FREE books?

Receive a slew of free Renee Rose books: Go to **http://subscribepage.com/alphastemp** to sign up for Renee Rose's newsletter and receive free books. In addition to the free stories and bonus material, you will also get special pricing, exclusive previews and news of new releases.

Download a free Lee Savino book from www. leesavino.com

Chapter One

Paloma

The moment the deadbolt to my bedroom door clicks into place, I dash for the closet.

Black clothes, so I won't be seen against the building at night. Flexible toe socks, so my toes can grip the rough-hewn stone of the mansion.

I quickly strip out of my "work" dress and into my escape gear.

I have an estimated three to eight minutes until they figure out how to get power back up, and in that time, I need to be out to the balcony, down the wall, and into the ocean where the security cameras won't pick me up, and thermoscans won't see my heat signature.

"You got this, you got this, you got this," I whisper-chant to myself as my trembling fingers draw the lock-picking tools out of the pouch. I'd stowed them in the pocket of these black yoga pants weeks ago after I caught the gardener's thirteen-year-old son picking a lock to the garage during one of my rare unguarded moments in the garden. Thom had sent me out for a walk after telling me I was overweight

1

and needed more exercise. I'd been thrilled to be allowed outside.

The boy told me he hadn't meant any harm and was just practicing his lock-picking skills. He'd shown me the instruction book and tool kit he ordered online. I said I would keep it between us, but I had to confiscate his instruction book and tools. Mean of me but necessary. I'll leave them in the flowerbed below my window. Maybe he'll find them someday.

I drop to my knees in front of the French doors to the balcony.

Slipping the slender tension wrench into the lock, I apply pressure to its plug. Then I slide in the pin. I close my eyes to concentrate. I've practiced this at least a hundred times. I already know how to find and set each pin, one at a time, until the lock fully disengages. With a little more pressure on the tension wrench, I turn the plug.

Click.

This is as far as I've ever gotten. I couldn't open the doors before because the electronic monitor at the top would notify Thom's security team that a door had been breached. Now, with the power cut to the property, I have a moment.

I let out an exhale, stow the tools in my pocket, and use both hands to pull the doors open.

They don't budge.

I scan the door frame. Did I miss something? A second lock? A physical bar or barrier? I don't see anything.

"Come on," I growl in an undertone. I pull harder.

It's not moving.

"*Juepucha,*" I mutter. "Come on, you bitch." I yank with all my strength. The doors fly open, and a gust of ocean breeze fills the room, making the curtains flap.

Yes!

My days as the girl in the tower are over. I slip out and silently shut the doors behind me.

You've heard the stories about girls in towers, right? Some of them are supposedly fair maidens. Some are princesses. Some have long hair that princes use as a climbing rope to save them.

Me? I guess I'm a mage of sorts. I can see the future of a company just by looking at its numbers.

Hence, my usefulness as a day trader.

I am also technically a maiden if that means virgin. The jury's out on the fair part. Does that mean good-looking or pale-skinned? I was never sure. Whatever. I'm Latinx, so I identify as BIPOC if anyone is wondering. And I'm not a size four. Not even close.

I throw a leg over the carved marble railing that brackets the balcony to straddle it, then the other, balancing my weight on the one-inch ledge that rims the outside.

Don't look down, I whisper.

My particular fairytale lacks the trellis for me to climb down, but metal wires run horizontally along the building to support the ivy. I lean out, wrap my toes around one of them, and test it with my weight. It holds.

Holding my breath, I transfer one hand to another wire. It cuts into my hands but serves. I leave the safety of the ledge and feel with my free foot for a wire below. It's farther than I expect, but I eventually catch it. Then I realize some of the ivy boughs might be thick enough to hold me.

That works better. I scale down, seeking the wires with my feet but sliding my hands along the thicker ivy cords. I'm three floors up, a distance that feels far higher and longer to scale now that I'm doing it. And I've already wasted too much time.

The lights could come back on any second now.

The branch I'm holding is too thin, and it breaks. I plunge downward, my fingers grasping for something else to hold and finally catching. My skin tears, and my fingers burn, but I barely notice. All my focus is on getting down.

I jump before I should, jarring my ankle and smacking my knee on the earth below. But it doesn't matter—I'm out. I take off running for the ocean as fast as I can.

I've been training for this, too. I may be on the heavy side, but every day, I race on my treadmill that faces the ocean, whispering to my body that the day will come when we can make a break for it. My illness makes it harder, but the medicine seems to be working.

I wasn't ready for it to be tonight. I wanted to locate Wren and make a plan to get her to safety before I escaped. Also, I need to figure out how to access the medicine keeping me alive. The last time I tried to escape, I collapsed before I could get far. But I'm feeling stronger now and don't have a choice. I'm out of time.

Thom let me in on his disgusting plan tonight at dinner.

Tomorrow night, he arranged to auction me and my trading services off to the highest bidder. It's not enough that I make him billions. He must sell me to one of his buddies to cement a high society merger. His twisted version of an arranged marriage.

Sorry, no. Not happening.

This time, my escape plan will work. It has to.

The mansion's lights come back on in a sudden blaze.

Dammit.

Run, run, run. I put my head down and sprint as fast as I can. My feet hit sand.

An alarm goes off. It will still take them time to realize I'm gone, hopefully. So long as–

"Hold it right there!" a male voice shouts.

No! I've been spotted.

I might still make it. I can hide in the water. I reach the shore and run in, diving into the freezing water before it's deep enough, so it's more of a belly flop. I use my hands on the rocks below to propel me into the deeper water.

I don't look behind me. I don't want to see how close they are. Whether they're coming for me. I squeeze my eyes closed and paddle hard, forgetting that I may not survive the ocean even if I'm not caught.

But I am caught.

A strong arm loops around my neck and shoves my head under, holding me down.

I struggle, kicking out, using my elbows, trying to duck out of his grasp. I need to take a breath.

Is this guy trying to kill me?

Clearly, he doesn't know that I'm the golden goose.

Everything's muffled by the sound of water around me, but I hear shouts above. Lights blaze in the periphery of my vision. Stars dance before my eyes.

And then I'm up. Held by my hair above water.

"What are you doing?" Thom rages from the shore.

"I'm sorry, Mr. Thompson. I thought she was an intruder."

"Get my daughter back to shore."

His *daughter.* Every time he calls me that I want to barf.

Chip, Thom's head of security, and another guard grab me by the arms and drag me forward, out of the ocean, onto the beach where Thom slaps me hard across the face.

I figure this is my one chance. If there's any man who works for Thom who has any conscience at all, I need to alert him. If he doesn't disobey now, maybe he'll raise a flag with the authorities.

"Let me go!" I scream. "You can't auction me off. I'm not your property! You can't keep me prisoner here forever!"

A needle jabs into the meaty part of my arm before I even see it coming. I stare into the eyes of the man who delivered it and detect a sadistic gleam of pleasure in them right before my vision goes dark, and my legs forget how to hold me.

* * *

Darius

Billionaires have a certain sort of smell. Not just clean human skin but the extra bouquet of expensive skin care products, rare perfumes, richer food.

That's what my bear thinks, anyway. After years living in Manhattan, my poor animal's nose has attuned to all sorts of city smells. It's a relief to helicopter to the Hamptons for the weekend, even if it is to rub elbows with the crustiest of Wall Street's upper crust. I step onto the tarmac and breathe my first clean lungful in months. The air tastes sweet with a tang of salt. Across a half-mile of manicured lawn, sunlight flashes on the wind-whipped sea.

The richer you are, the more land you can afford. My host, Thom Thompson, learned about my successful real estate investment firm, Medvedev Enterprises, and my new hedge fund, Mountain Top Investments, and invited me to this long weekend, so he can introduce me to potential clients. Thom owns a massive estate on the water between wildlife preserves.

Woods, my bear points out. He wants to strip off my human skin and lumber into the wild. Keeping him caged in has been the hardest part about living in Manhattan. These woods are nothing like the wilderness of Bad Bear Mountain where I grew up, but it's enough to remind me of what I'm missing now that I've made New York City my home.

No, I tell him. I can't release him here. He doesn't get to go romping around in a pine forest like my brothers and I used to on Bad Bear Mountain. He doesn't get to run wild at all. Not after what he did. He can't be trusted.

I check my collar and shoot my cuffs. I'm in my best off-hours blazer, designed to look casual while still perfectly tailored. My loafers are handmade in a small village outside of Milan. I'm groomed head to toe to fit in with the humans I'll be networking with all weekend, the one percent of the one percent.

My one unruly feature is my thick blond hair. I get it cut every week, but I swear my bear makes it grow faster to spite me. The wind tousles it as I stride from the helicopter.

"This way, sir." An estate staff member in a navy blue uniform takes my suitcase and guides me towards a mansion that would make Great Gatsby turn green. I brace myself, expecting the place to smell old, like oiled wood and ancient horsehair furniture, but the inside is modern.

The owner and the man who invited me is waiting in the foyer to greet all his guests. "Darius, welcome."

"Mr. Thompson." I shake his hand, careful not to use too much pressure. A firm handshake from a bear shifter would crush a human's bones.

"Please, call me Thom," he says in a reedy voice. He's casually dressed in an outfit that costs more than a new car.

"Thanks for inviting me."

"Of course, my boy." Thom and I have met a handful of times, but he's the sort who fancies himself a mentor. He makes a show of taking younger men under his wing, giving himself credit for their success, and discarding them the second they fall from grace. "I'm sure you'll find this weekend instructive." He doesn't let me get a word in, so I settle for murmuring my appreciation as he continues. "Lockepoint has several pools and tennis courts. And the golf course. I hope we'll be able to get a few rounds in tomorrow. They tell me it might rain." He frowns as if the weather is an employee who needs a reprimand. Wealth can insulate a person from any inconvenience, but nature is nature.

"I'm just happy to be out of the city."

"Yes, I'm so glad you could come to my humble abode." The *humble abode* he's talking about has almost thirty bedrooms. It's over a hundred thousand square feet, not including the guest and pool houses. "Nester will show you to your room, but don't linger. Cocktails will be served here until six, and then we will sit down for dinner."

More guests arrive, so I thank him and move on, following Nester up two flights of stairs and down a long hallway to a room with windows that overlook the ocean.

Let me out.

My bear is still clamoring to get out into the woods.

I placate him by opening the windows to clear the smell of billionaire. I throw each of them open and breathe in the ocean air. A breeze ruffles my hair. I swear it grows another centimeter as I stand there.

My phone buzzes, and I check the screen. It's Teddy, my twin. "Fuck off," I mutter and send it to voicemail. We may be identical, but we're as different as two brothers could be. He joined the military at age eighteen, a special ops unit for shifters, and embraces his base animal nature. I stuffed my bear away and moved to New York.

Someone had to earn the money to support our family on Bad Bear Mountain.

My phone buzzes again. This time it's Lana, my brother's human mate. I frown. Maybe something's wrong. When I answer, though, it's Teddy's voice on the other side.

"What the fuck, D-bag. You answer for her but not me?" he accuses me without a greeting.

"Teddy," Lana admonishes from somewhere close by. She's the sunshine to his grump. "He might be working."

"I *am* working, actually." I would cuss Teddy out, but Lana's on the call. I like Lana. She's nice. "What do you want?"

"We're wondering if you're coming to the mountain for Thanksgiving."

"Aww, *Medvezhonok*," I use my nickname for my brother. He hates it almost as much as he hates his full name, Theodore. "Miss me?"

"Not at all, asshole. This is about Lana. She's planning a big family dinner. You need to come home."

"Bad Bear Mountain is not my home. New York is." Last time I visited Bad Bear Mountain, I vowed I'd never return. It brings out my bear urges, and I can't afford the danger that creates.

Teddy scoffs. "Come home."

I frown. My bear twists and turns inside me, struggling to get free. I shove him down. "I don't think I can make it."

"Give me the phone," Lana orders. Teddy grumbles something, but she's got him wrapped around her finger, so the next thing I hear is Lana's sweet voice. "Okay, that wasn't going well. Let's try this again. Hi, Darius!"

My lips quirk at my sister-in-law's infinite cheeriness. I'm not attracted to Lana, but I'd be lying if I didn't admit I'm jealous as hell that my idiot brother found his mate.

Even if I moved in circles with other bears or if fate matched me with a human and I managed to find her, I couldn't possibly mate. My bear is too unstable. He destroys everything he touches. I can't let him out.

"Hi, Lana."

"Listen, will you please, please, please, please come home for Thanksgiving? It's really important to me."

"Why?" It's a dick thing to say, and Lana doesn't deserve me being an asshole to her, especially not when it's her company's wealth that ended up saving Bad Bear Mountain before I got Mountain Top and its real estate investment subsidiary, Medvedev Investments, to a nine-figure company.

"We have some news if you must know." Her voice softens.

I don't know why it hits me like a punch to the gut.

Teddy's going to have a cub.

The news ignites a thread of loneliness deep inside me. The pull of family and the mountain competing with my drive to succeed here.

Except there's no need for me to earn billions anymore. The need disappeared when Teddy mated Lana. I was doing everything to save the mountain, including trying to develop it so we could keep it from falling into the hands of another cutthroat hedge fund. Teddy sees me as another evil hedge fund bro, but I was going to use my powers for good, dammit.

But Lana's money kept the outsiders out. Without development.

I'm useless to the family I alienated myself from and worked so hard to rescue.

"That's great," I find myself saying hollowly. "Congratulations." I want to end the conversation. "Yeah, I'll try to be there, Lana."

"Don't just try," Lana shows a hint of steel that makes

her a successful businesswoman in her own right. "Make it happen, Darius."

"Okay, Lana." I know when I've been out-negotiated. "I have to go. But I'll keep you posted."

"Make it happen," she repeats. I end the call and sigh.

I look in the mirror and grumble at my hair, which grew *another* centimeter while I was on the call. My bear's protest at me refusing to go home.

I have to go back downstairs. I'm here to network, and that bullshit takes place over cocktails and dinner.

I head down to the reception room where a server takes my drink order, and I carry my whiskey on the rocks over to the fireplace.

There's a massive oil painting of Thom over the mantel. He's in a striking pose, with a younger woman seated by his side. My eyes are immediately drawn to her perfect oval face. Dark hair, dark eyes, plump lips. Her skin is a few shades darker than Thom's pasty complexion.

Maybe it's just my longing for a mate like Lana, but I'm drawn to the portrait. She's the most stunning female I've ever seen. The painter must have been a little in love with her. She's too beautiful to be real.

I did my research on the host before coming here and didn't find any evidence that Thom was ever married. The woman is probably his partner, but she's young enough to be his daughter. She doesn't look old enough to be out of college, but I've met plenty of men who prefer trophy wives in their twenties.

No, my bear makes his displeasure known. I ignore him. He's been increasingly unhappy with everyone and everything. Living in the city around so many people is hard on him. I work over a hundred hours a week. He misses my brothers and the mountain. He wants freedom.

But I don't dare let him out. Every time I do, it's been a disaster.

The grand receiving room fills with people. There are a few older men who look like Thom plus a fresh crop of frat boy-types with weak chins, strong cologne, and expensive watches bought with Daddy's money. The room reeks of entitlement.

These are the people I'm supposed to schmooze with all weekend. For most people, a few days lounging in a mansion with the ultra rich would be a dream come true but not for me. There's nothing relaxing about glad-handing humans all day and convincing them to invest in my company.

But I didn't build Mountain Top Investments from nothing without sacrifice. Thom Thompson owns the most successful hedge fund in the world. I'm here to learn his secrets and see if he was serious about partnering with my investment firm for a real estate deal.

I toss back my drink and prepare to wade into the fray. Before I do, the scent of hothouse flowers catches my attention. It's coming from the nearby hall. I wander that way and stop short at the sight of a woman descending the grand staircase. She's short and curvy with pillowy lips and shining hair.

It's the young woman from the painting. I was wrong. The painter didn't exaggerate the flawless balance of her features. She's fifty times as stunning in real life. My bear surges under my skin.

She descends slowly, scanning the room. She's dressed in a modest white dress that makes her golden skin glow. Halfway down, she catches me staring, and her lovely dark eyes narrow with a glare. Her scent blooms for me, orchids and gardenias, with a bitter undertone.

My chest rumbles as my bear tries to voice his opinions. He's as transfixed as I am, but unhappy with the medicinal edge of her scent. I step back, grunting to cover my bear's growl, and rub my breastbone to settle him. For one millisecond, he gets control. I almost spontaneously shift the way I did as a child–far too young and completely out of control. I shove him back down with ferocious will.

Damn.

The momentary loss of control must be a combination of being out here in the woods and seeing the first female I've been attracted to in a long time. I will have to be careful this weekend. I can't have my bear fighting me every time I get a hard-on for a pretty female.

The woman reaches the bottom step, and two hulking men in black suits and clear earpieces step forward to flank her. She lifts her chin to a haughty angle and heads the direction they point. Two more men fall into step behind them.

She looks and acts like a spoiled socialite, but something about the way her bodyguards hover upsets my bear.

No.

He doesn't like those men near her. He's never been so vocal. Once again, he wrestles me for control, and only years of subduing him allow me to keep the upper hand.

What the fuck is happening?

I stalk through the doorway, keeping the woman in my sights. This settles my bear. She's standing beside Thompson now, silent and pouting. They had a tiff, perhaps. Her sugar daddy didn't give her the Mercedes she wanted.

When we all head to the dining room for dinner, the bodyguards surround her again. One of them holds the chair out for her, like he's a combination bodyguard / butler, and she sinks into the seat opposite the head of the table.

Something makes me slide into the seat beside her, and she gives me another cold look. She smells wrong—like medicine. Is she sick? Up close, I note the dark circles under her eyes. They're not enough to diminish her beauty but could be a sign of poor sleep. Perhaps a headache. That would explain the bad temper.

Thompson stands at the head of the table and clears his throat. "Thank you all for coming." He paces around the table, like he's our school master teaching us a lesson. "This will be a weekend to remember."

Everyone murmurs their assent.

He stops behind the young woman's chair. "And I'm so pleased to present my daughter, Paloma, to you all." He places a hand on her shoulder.

Daughter. My research didn't tell me Thom had any children. He must have worked hard to keep that information under the radar.

I study Paloma's face for any hint that she's related to Thom but can't find any. Her mother must have been a rare beauty with dominant genes.

"She's been working hard at her trader position with Thompson Capital, but I convinced her to take some time off," Thom continues. "She's done great things at the firm, and I'm so proud of her." There's a smattering of polite applause.

Paloma doesn't appear moved by his praise. If anything, it seems to deaden her.

Thompson picks up his daughter's hand and kisses it. Her expression never changes. She stares straight ahead as if in silent protest.

If Thompson notices her attitude, he doesn't seem to

care. "By the end of the weekend, I might have another announcement regarding a merger of a more personal variety."

More applause, this time louder, with an eager edge. A few of the older businessmen lean in and whisper something to their younger counterparts. "...bidding...tomorrow night..." I hear one say. My shifter hearing is sharp enough to pick up on the words, but they make no sense.

What did Thompson mean by a merger of a more personal variety? Something's going on.

Thompson proposes a toast to his daughter. We all raise our glasses. Paloma doesn't move to take her glass, and one bodyguard leans over her and prods her arm.

That's when I notice the purple marks marring her skin between shoulder and elbow. They look like someone grabbed her arm and gripped hard. She lifts her wine glass, and her dress sleeve falls away, revealing more bruises.

My bear rears up. Once more, I almost spontaneously shift. My bear's going crazy, wanting to burst from my skin. Damn, after all these years living in New York City, I thought I'd learned to suppress that wildness. I blink at my plate, hoping to hide any brightness in my eyes. My fangs sharpen, and I grit my teeth, forcing my bear to retreat. *Stay back*, I tell him.

I force myself to focus on eating, but it's a struggle not to watch Paloma. Three courses in, I dare to look at her again. She's sitting with that hardened look on her beautiful face. If I hadn't seen the bruises, I might think her snobbish.

But now I think it's a result of abuse.

Her head bodyguard leans forward again. "Eat," he orders her. She subtly shakes her head, but he reaches over her and cuts her steak like she's a child. He forks a piece of meat and holds it in front of her lips.

A muscle clenches in her jaw. "No," she mutters. "I'm not hungry."

"*Stop.*" There's bear in my growl. My outburst attracts the table's attention.

Paloma's gaze jerks to me.

Thom and his conversation partners go silent. I half rise out of my chair before I know what's going on. I face off with the bodyguard. "The lady said no."

Paloma locks eyes with me and a current of energy runs between us. "I *did* say no." She sounds surprised that I heard and heeded her no. Which is fucked up. Thom must be a controlling bastard.

"It's getting late. Perhaps you're tired," Thom says to his daughter. He doesn't wait for her to respond. "Take her to her room." He gestures to her bodyguards. The same asshole who was trying to feed her draws her chair back and takes her limp arm to guide her away. She glances back at me over her shoulder as she walks out.

Does she want me to intercede? My bear roars to life. He is apparently ready to kill on her behalf. Not a normal reaction for the animal I have kept caged since I was a teenager.

I forcibly keep him down, tightening my muscles to keep from jumping from my chair to follow her.

My alarm bells clang. No one else seems to think it was odd, but I am weirded out by the whole interaction between Thom's unhappy daughter and her controlling bodyguards.

Something rotten is going on in this mansion, and I intend to figure out what.

Chapter Two

Paloma

P I expect to find myself locked in my bedroom all day while so many guests are in the mansion, but the deadbolt slides open at six a.m.–the same time it does every morning. I assume I'm free to follow my normal Saturday routine.

Thom probably figures he instilled enough fear in me to keep me in line.

He'd be right.

After my escape attempt the night before last, Thom told me point blank that if I didn't fall into line and do everything he told me to do, Wren would meet a horrible accident. *A horrible accident like our parents'.*

I wasn't sure until then that he'd been the one responsible for their death. That it hadn't been a random car accident. Now I know for certain–he orchestrated it to get me under his roof.

He's as horrible a man as I suspected.

The first few years under his guardianship hadn't been

bad. Wren and I were grieving, but he provided us with every luxury, including a therapist to help us cope.

A therapist I now realize brainwashed us to be his little robots.

I rebelled when he pulled me out of school to work long hours. That's when he sent Wren away to a Catholic boarding school where she's not allowed a cell phone or unsupervised internet. He made my contact with her a punishment or reward. I misbehaved, Thom revoked my privilege of my weekly video call with her. If I wanted her to come home for Christmas, I'd better keep my quotas up.

What he doesn't know is that Wren has a special knack for psychic linking. Sometimes when I'm falling asleep at night, she appears in my dream state, checking in on me. Telling me a joke. Acting like a goofy seventeen-year-old. If I didn't have those moments with her, I would go nuts.

I have to be careful he never finds out, though, or he'll think of some devious way to put her gift to use as well.

I pull on my khaki riding jodhpurs and a fitted red top, don my boots and hat, and head to the stables to see Starlight. Riding her is the only pleasure I have here. Starlight and Sunday video calls with Wren.

My mare whinnies softly when I open the door.

"Hey, sweetness. I missed you yesterday." I look over my shoulder at the two bodyguards trailing me. "They wouldn't let me out to see you." I stroke her forehead and lean forward. "*Pendejos*," I murmur in her silky ear.

I still swear in Spanish—despite Thom's disgust of it—because it reminds me of my dad—my *real* dad—who spoke English at home except when he swore. I'm sure that it was to protect our delicate ears, but instead, he just taught us to swear in his native tongue.

Cas, the Dutch groom, appears at my back, carrying her

saddle. "I'll get her ready for you, Miss Paloma," he murmurs, avoiding my eyes.

I like Cas, but I have to be honest. He's not my friend. Everyone who works at this mansion knows I'm a prisoner, and no one has lifted a finger to help me.

Then again, Thom probably holds something over each of their heads. A pressure point he pushes on to ensure their ongoing cooperation.

Had he done that with my mom when she worked for him? Had he pressured her to do things she didn't want to do? Did he kill her because she wouldn't give him access to exploit me?

I fasten the chin strap on my helmet as Cas leads Starlight out of her stall.

"All set, Miss Paloma. I'll bring her out for you."

"Thank you, Cas." I follow them outside then climb the stair to mount.

I throw my leg over Starlight and take the reins. In the early days of Thom's guardianship, Wren and I got exposure to all the rich kid extracurriculars. Archery, yachting, fencing, and of course riding lessons. We even had an English riding instructor come out to train us. I learned dressage and even had dreams of competing with Starlight. But Thom decided that would take away from my "studies."

Of course, my studies had completely become stock market related. The tutor didn't even come anymore for a pretense of home school. Every waking moment was focused on studying the numbers and making trades.

I've always been able to sense a company's future success or failure. Which markets were ready to flourish and which were withering on the vine. It was easy.

My mother noticed my ability first. She called it a gift.

She never lived to see it become a curse that's turned my life into a nightmare.

Over the years, I've made Thom billions. But it's not enough. It's never enough. Thom owns me. If he has his way, he'll control me for the rest of his life, and now he plans to make me work for his friends, too.

There's nothing I can do about it.

I guide Starlight to trot the familiar path to the beach. Once we're there, overlooking the wild, choppy sea, I loosen the reins and prompt her into a canter, then a gallop. Spray flies, spattering my perfect outfit. Starlight thunders over the sand, racing the wind. My hair streams behind me like a flag.

It's not freedom, but it's the closest thing to it I can get. I savor every second.

I'm halfway down the long stretch of surf when Starlight shies and startles. I slow us down, so I can coax her to quiet. She's nervous, prancing, but I don't know why. We're far from the guard posts that mark the end of Thom's land, and she's used to the security teams patrolling the dunes with their guns, making sure I don't run.

Then I see the swimmer in the water. It's too cold to be in the ocean–as I know only too well from the night before last. Only an idiot would jump into these waters for pleasure without a wetsuit, but there he is, big and bare-chested, shaking his dark blond hair out of his face, striding out of the waves. Water streams down the epic muscles of his shoulders and chest. I'm instantly reminded of the hundreds of historical romance novels Ellie has slipped me over the years. He could easily be on the cover of one.

He looks like a Viking, striding onshore to kill and plunder. And he's headed straight toward me.

I instantly recognize him–he's the man who sat beside

me last night at dinner. The one who told that asshole Chip to stop force-feeding me. I was drawn to him immediately, despite the fact that if he was at that dinner, then he must be here to bid on me.

The wind chafes my face, and my fingers are frozen, but the rest of my body heats. I try to look away from his glistening wet chest, but I can't.

He's...incredible. Light glistens over his great pectoral muscles, where rivulets of water stream down to the narrowed "V" of his waist.

Seeing him stokes a fire in my lower belly, which grows to an all-consuming blaze. I've probably been around too many milquetoast boys of good breeding because I've never been attracted to a man like this. Maybe that's the difference. They were boys, and this is a man, wild, with eyes like the stormy sea.

"Good morning." He lifts his hand to wave and starts toward the shore. His voice is a deep rumble. It only increases the jump of excitement in my belly. My inner thighs squeeze against Starlight.

She doesn't like him. She dances backward, shaking her head. Only years of riding keep me in my saddle. It doesn't help that my legs have gone weak.

"Is it?" I call back as Starlight whirls in a circle.

The Viking halts waist-deep in the water, studying me as he rubs the golden stubble on his chin. His hair looks longer than it did last night. Despite the decidedly masculine lines of a rugged jaw and bushy brows, his lips are full and perfect. What would it be like to kiss a man with a beard?

Why am I staring at this man's lips? And why am I wondering what it would be like if he won the bid for me? But I do wonder. Of course, my engagement will be fake.

Thom is just lending me out for my "gift." This man wouldn't be a real fiancé. He wouldn't expect any kind of marital rights.

But what if he did?

What if he tossed me over his shoulder, carried me out to the beach, and ravished me right here on the sand? I'd get away and run like I did the other night. He wouldn't send my bodyguards after me; he'd chase me himself. And when he caught me...

Oh damn. I have definitely read far too many of the Viking, Regency, and Highlander romance novels Ellie got me hooked on.

I try to shake off the fizzy excitement that thought brings. I must be nuts if I'm fantasizing about how Thom's plans to loan me out like a work slave to a fictitious fiancé will play out for me. This isn't a sexy Viking come to carry me off to a foreign land. He wants to buy me and use me like Thom uses me to increase his coffers.

I touch my heels to Starlight's side and let her have her head, so she can get us away. As I ride, I sense his gaze on my straight back, and it takes everything I have not to look back.

* * *

Darius

I watch Paloma race her horse away from me like the hounds of hell are following. For a moment, our gaze connected, and I felt lightning sizzle between us. I almost shifted again.

My bear is apparently in love.

But a moment later, she was gone.

My blood pumps, and not just from my brisk swim.

22

Seeing Paloma revs my heartbeat. Her lovely face, her rosebud pout. My dick is hard and ready, even while the rest of me is numb from the freezing water.

Her. Now, my bear says. He wants to go after her. Her horse was panicking at my strange bear shifter smell, and getting closer might mean the horse would spook and throw Paloma off. I want to get close to Paloma to get to know her when she's relaxed and free of her guards, where she feels safe enough to tell me how she got the ugly bruises on her arms.

Last night, I spent interminable hours choking on cigar smoke and bland conversation with the rest of the guests. I learned Paloma was born to a couple who worked as traders in Thom's firm. They died in a car crash when she was fourteen, and Thom became her guardian. She's adopted, like me. But if there was ever any love between her and the man who calls himself her father, it's gone now.

I tried to dig more, to figure out what mergers Thom might be planning, so I can learn more about the bidding I heard whispers about, but nobody said anything.

I didn't get to poke around the way I wanted. Today, I'll use my heightened sense of smell and hearing to do some sleuthing, starting with finding out more about the tragic and enigmatic beauty surrounded by bodyguards.

After dressing in my room, I stroll through the halls like I own the place. This is how rich people behave. They push and shoulder their way into whatever place they desire, with the sheer belief that they belong anywhere they choose to go. It's like the animal world with a show of dominance, except you never know what they have for teeth and claws.

My nose tells me that Thom's rooms are in the west wing. I head that way, poking my head into random rooms, trying door handles. I'm looking for an office.

A heavy door stymies my way to the west wing. It's locked, and there's a black keypad beside it. Thom has taken the precaution of extra security, which is a good sign I'm in the right place.

I open a window. I'm on the second story, and it only takes a moment to leap from one windowsill to a small balcony. An impossible feat for a human, but no problem for a werebear who spent his childhood climbing trees. No one's on the grounds, but I duck down anyway, and use my sharp claws to carve into the glass. No alarms sound, and I can reach a hand through the hole to open the French door.

Just like that, I'm past security and in the wing that holds Thom's private offices. If I'm lucky, I'll uncover some secrets.

I slip out of the first room and head down the wide hall. I have to tread more carefully here. I catch the scent of guards–stale cigarettes and the faint smell of gunpowder– and a whiff of Thom's cologne.

Ten doors down, I hit the jackpot. Someone murmurs behind the closed door, and they sound a lot like Thom.

I lean my shoulder against a wall, half obscured by a marble plinth holding a rearing bull statue.

It's definitely Thom, speaking in his reedy voice. "Drink?" There's the clink of glass.

Then someone else says, "We could avoid all this business. Just make the deal now."

"Who would she be marrying?" Thom asks. "You?" He scoffs. "I want to avoid suspicion, not stoke it."

"Not me–my son. Chad will play the part of a suitable fiance. You get your money, I'll get access to her for three years–"

Access? What kind of sick transaction are they discussing?

24

"One. The deal is one. It's more than enough time for her to increase your holdings."

Oh. Not sex, then. Something else.

Let me out! My chest rumbles as my bear thrashes to get free, responding to this disgusting conversation. They're talking about selling Paloma off into a brief marriage so she can...what? Increase their wealth somehow?

"Very well. One year, and then Chad will call the engagement off. You'll be free to sell her again." Thom murmurs something I don't catch because someone brushes against the other side of the wall.

I wait.

"No," Thom barks. "I promised I wouldn't accept any preemptive bids. You and Chad can join the auction tonight. Midnight."

The other man protests, but Thom talks over him. "I'm being more than generous." Footsteps approach the door. "Now, let's be off. I'm late for my tee time."

The door handle scrapes, and I saunter off, turning casually into a small hallway before Thom and his conspirator exit the office. I catch the cigar fumes and scent of rare whiskey.

I listen, hoping Thom heads the opposite way. Instead, the footsteps get closer. The hall behind me leads to a small flight of stairs, and I trot down them to hide. Thom and his friend pass the door, still chatting about golf. They head off without noticing me.

I hover on the stairs, listening to their receding footfalls, when I get a whiff of something floral. Paloma's gardenia scent wafts up the stairs, and I can't help following it to the subterranean floor where it leads. The scent is thick and sweet but with that same bitter tang that alarmed me this morning and last night. The further I descend, the more the

25

bitterness overtakes the sweetness until a metallic flavor coats my tongue.

The stairs lead to another hallway. There's a hum behind the walls and the air is cooler. I'm probably near a server room or something.

Paloma's scent leads me to an open door. The room beyond is filled with massive screens. There's a small desk and chair where her scent is concentrated.

Paloma spends a lot of time here, and I think I know what she's doing. I bet if I flip the wall switch, the screens will light up with familiar numbers from the stock exchanges around the world. Thom said she works for his investment firm. I bet she uses this room to do her trading.

That's how she increases Thom's wealth. Thom and whoever he auctions her off to.

But why? He must have hundreds of traders available. What need would he have to use or sell his foster daughter? What's so special about what she does? Something illegal, perhaps?

Whatever it is, I feel sick.

I'm certain Paloma is a captive, held against her will by the billionaire who made himself her parent.

That explains why the door locks from the outside. I can smell the places her guards stand.

Has she tried to escape? Fought back? That could be how she got the bruises.

My bear is ready to rampage and rip this entire room apart. It's all I can do not to shift right there.

Instead, I make myself exit and shut the door. I have nothing to gain by losing control. I need to learn more, so I can decide if and how I can help Paloma.

* * *

Paloma

Ellie finishes curling my hair and stands back to survey her work. "Beautiful, as always."

Ellie is my—what do I call her? If we are staying with the fairytale nomenclature, she'd be my chambermaid or servant. I guess she's a combination jailer/personal assistant. She brings me food on a tray when Thom or his henchman Chip lock me in my chambers. She orders my clothing, trims my hair, and makes sure I have a fresh toothbrush. Last night she did my make up and hair, and she's going all out for tonight's masquerade ball. Thom invited seventy-five additional guests in for tonight's fête—another chance to show off, I guess.

I'm wearing a white strapless chiffon and silk jumper. I suspect it's supposed to evoke both "sweet innocence" and "bad-ass trader" at the same time.

The corset-like bustier top is heart-shaped to frame my breasts, and it connects in front to the matching wide-legged pants. A sheer fabric covers the shell and gives it an ethereal quality. A filmy wrap hangs over my arms to cover the bruises. Ellie smears a ginger-scented lotion over all of my exposed skin that leaves a shimmer.

I look at my reflection in the mirror, but I hardly recognize the young woman looking back at me. I've been locked in a tower for ten years now. Most of the time, I still feel like the grieving fourteen-year-old who first came here. The girl who'd rather curl up in her room and hide than interact with the world.

Carajo, I made it so easy for him.

"It's going to be all right," Ellie murmurs although it most certainly will not be.

I try to swallow and nod. "Sure."

Whatever awaits me tomorrow, I find it impossible to

believe it will be any better than what I have here. I won't just be changing one jailer for another. I'll be *bred*.

At least Thom has never had an interest in me sexually. I work for him—he keeps Wren safe and out of it. That's our agreement.

I glance at the picture of Wren stuck in the border of the mirror. I have photos of her everywhere to remind me why I must persevere. She's safe, for now. She's at a Catholic boarding school in Connecticut. One that doesn't allow cell phones or internet unless strictly supervised. It's the modern-day version of a medieval convent. I'm allowed a video call with her on Sundays unless my trades haven't been as profitable as Thom wants, in which case my sister is told I'm working late, and I'm locked in my room for the weekend.

The market took a dump Friday, but I managed to meet my quotas. I should be allowed a call with her tomorrow unless my new husband takes me before then.

Until this morning, he was a faceless replica of Thom.

Now, though, I find myself picturing the Viking from the beach.

A man who could probably snap my neck with one squeeze of those giant ham-hands. What if Thom sells me to him? What if he wanted...*more* than my stock trades?

Heat rolls down my inner thighs. What if he's rough?

A trembling starts in my legs. It's fear, not arousal. Definitely not arousal.

"A little more lip gloss." Ellie grabs a tube and swipes the wand of clear plumping gloss across my lips, even though I thought they were already quite moist. She surveys her work once more. "Perfect."

I don't enlist Ellie's help. I tried once, years ago, and she grew terrified. Tears streaked her face, and she begged me not to speak of it again.

"I can't help you," she'd whispered.

I figured Thom had some leverage over her, too. Something to keep her in line, same as he keeps me in line. So to spare her–my only "friend" here now that Wren is gone–I don't make a fuss.

I glance at the clock. "I still have fifteen minutes. I'm going to read." I crawl up on my four-poster with no consideration of whether I wrinkle my virgin business woman outfit.

Ellie opens her mouth to argue, but I've already picked up *The Spymaster's Lady*, the Joanna Bourne romance I'm reading for the seventh time. She closes her mouth again. "Of course. I'll see you later." She slips out the door.

Usually on weekends, I spend as much time outside as I can, since my weekdays are spent in a work dungeon with only blue light from the monitors. Today I had no desire to rub elbows with my suitors, though. Suitors is probably not an apt term, even if I am living a fairytale nightmare. My would-be owners? Jailors?

Anyway, after my morning ride, I spent the rest of the day voluntarily locked in my chambers, reading. Escapism is the best I can hope for.

Escapism and...

I'm not hoping for the Viking to be the winner. I definitely *don't* want a man like that.

Okay, maybe I do. He's the least like my foster father of all of them, at least in appearance. He took that giant, muscled body into the cold ocean this morning *for fun*. And he defended me last night.

But he's still a horrible human engaging in human trafficking and forced labor. Of course, he might not understand the extent of Thom's control over me. Maybe he thinks I'm willing. That I profit from the deal, too.

A light tap sounds on my door, and I tense before it opens, knowing who will be there.

I'm already swinging my legs off the bed to stand when Thom walks in.

"Ah. Darling." He spreads his arms in my direction. "You look magnificent."

"Not your darling," I say through clenched teeth.

He drops the fatherly pretense. "Remember what we talked about," he warns. "I didn't care for your lifeless act last night." He cups my chin, and I wrench back, out of his grasp.

"I did everything you asked of me," I seethe.

He nods. "You did. And you'd better continue to do so, or Wren will suffer the consequences."

Hot tears spear my eyes. "Leave her out of this. That's all I ever ask of you."

He smiles, like he's pleased he won my tears. "And I have upheld my end of the bargain. You are the one who tried to flee."

My nose burns. I clench my fists so tightly my nails dig into my palms. "It won't happen again," I say stiffly.

"Good." He beckons to me. "Now, put on your mask. I expect you to make a better impression than you did last night. I'm not just leasing your services to your new fiance."

Alarm bells go off. The room swoops around me. Cold rushes through my limbs. Somehow, I know that whatever he means, it's going to be terrible.

"What are you talking about?" I don't keep the warble out of my voice.

"The highest bidder will also take your virginity, darling. We've kept you locked away from men for far too

30

long," he says as he ties the mask on. "It's high time I breed you to see if my grandchildren are equally as talented."

I catch the wall to keep from falling over. Now the cold turns to hot, like hot iron pouring down through the top of my head and into my chest, creating a terrible rushing in my ears.

Thom's lips twist into a satisfied smile at my reaction. He picks up the masquerade mask and walks around behind me to put it on.

I should run. I should dive out the window and break my neck rather than give him the satisfaction of breeding me.

Except for Wren. I can't go off half-cocked until I have a plan to get her to safety. I can't risk him pulling her out of school to do the same horrifying things to her.

The silk of the mask drapes over my eyes, and he ties it in the back. My hairs stand on end at having the devil so close to me.

Chapter Three

Darius

Thom's masquerade ball isn't just for the house guests. He invited an extended list of friends and acquaintances to join the party tonight. Starting at dusk, a never-ending line of Lamborghinis, Bugattis, and Rolls Royces convenes on the mansion. I pick up the flimsy black mask a staff member delivered a few minutes ago. It'll go well with my black on black tux. I look like James Bond, but I can't shake my apprehension.

Tonight, I intend to find out what's going on with Paloma. There's something wrong here. I don't have proof, but I know it in my gut.

My bear wants to rampage. After years of keeping the upper hand, I'm tested now by his uprising. When I glance in the mirror, my eyes are golden. I have to fight to get my bear under control, so my eyes return to their human color. Only threatening to stay in my room gets him to recede. He wants to see Paloma. If it were up to him, I wouldn't let her out of my sight.

But I'm not an uncivilized Neanderthal. When I was

young, I was a wild child, almost feral. I've spent years building up my control, and I'm not about to lose my head.

I shaved my face clean earlier, but when I exit my bedroom, I have a beard. My bear's way of rebelling. I'll allow it, as long as he knows his place.

I saunter into the ballroom, accepting a glass of champagne. Thom must have hired a whole agency of models to attend because there are tall and attractive women everywhere I look. The models tower over the frat boys, who all look like Christmas has come early. The rest of the crowd is the bored, rich set who live in the Hamptons. I float through them, nodding at people I know through business. I keep it moving, waiting to catch the gardenia scent.

Paloma enters the room surrounded by a flock of bodyguards. They keep multiplying. Soon she'll have better security than a president.

I move closer to get a better glimpse of her. She's in white again, her lush breasts pushed up and framed in a strapless top. The color makes her glow like a goddess. Even with the mask hiding those big expressive eyes, it's clear she's the loveliest woman in the room.

There's a queue of country club types forming a line beside her. The band strikes up, and I don't need my shifter hearing to know that she's being induced to dance. A man twice her age leads her out to the dance floor. She dances with him, and halfway through the song, the next man cuts in and claims her. Then the next. There's no surprise on her face when each new partner arrives. There's no pretense of enjoyment, either. She doesn't make much conversation with any of them. It's almost as if it's prearranged—who she will dance with and when. As if this is Paloma's coming out party, and she's now available on the marriage market.

Was that the merger Thompson was referring to?

I pass a white-haired man scolding his son. "Focus. We need to win the auction."

The son protests and gets rapped by his father's cane.

"–Tonight, midnight. After that, you can do as you like." The father prods the son forward, and he reluctantly heads across the room towards Paloma.

"–Sample the merchandise," another man in the apparent queue mutters.

My bear nearly forces his way out. I want to smash my champagne glass on the ground, tear off my suit, and destroy anyone who dares touch her.

Instead, I get a giant glass of merlot and stroll to the center of the floor, where a thirty-year-old guy with a seventy thousand dollar watch and a receding hairline is attempting to steer Paloma through the other dancers. Without bothering to pretend to trip, I toss my drink on him. The dark liquid spatters all over his front and soaks into the expensive Italian cotton.

"Oops," I say.

The man curses. Paloma steps back. Her white jumper escaped any stains.

Her dance partner starts to bluster, and I catch his gaze, holding it until he sees the ferocity of my bear and drops his eyes. "You'd better go change." I arch my brow. "I'll take over from here." I step in front of him and take Paloma's hand, then tug her into my arms.

Her sweet scent surrounds me, and for a moment, I'm dizzy. The bitter tang has receded, and I can smell only her delectable skin, along with a light scent of ginger. I want to lick up her neck and taste her properly.

"May I have this dance?" I give her my most dazzling smile and maneuver us into the waltz my mother Winnie taught us when we were gangly teens.

"Oh, now he asks."

I can't tell if she's flirting or annoyed.

I'm not the grouchy and stand-offish bear type like my brother, Teddy. I learned to schmooze and charm humans to win on this cut-throat playing field. But, for the first time, I'm unsure of myself. For the first time, I actually care whether my charm lands or not.

Paloma matches me step for step, leaning on me and responding to the slightest pressure. We twist and turn together, dancing like we were born to do it.

"Don't tell me you preferred your old partner."

"Chinless Chad? No."

I bark a laugh, but she lifts a shoulder. "I prefer to be left alone." Despite her words, her gaze roams my face with what I hope is interest.

"Yes. It looks like you have a long line of suitors." I glance over to see her former dance partner's father angrily speaking to her retinue of guards.

She mutters something in Spanish.

"I'm sorry?"

She lifts her chin. "Underneath all that muscle you must actually be a very small man."

Wow. Okay, now it's getting personal. I'm not sure what I did to inspire this attack, but my bear likes that she can give it back. Last night I imagined her to be cowed by her foster father and his men.

"I don't know, most women find me to be more than adequate in, ah, *that* department." I flick my brows above the mask.

Her bodyguards surround the dance floor. Two of them shoulder their way through the dancers on the floor toward us.

What in the ever-loving fuck is going on here? Does

Thom not realize what spectacle his men are making in front of his Hampton guests? Does he not care?

A flush appears on her cheeks and throat from my innuendo. She attempts to pull away, but I keep her against my body, loving the feel of her soft curves. I turn our bodies, dancing away from the approaching guards.

"You disgust me." Her nostrils flare. "Any man who bids on a woman's virginity must have *deep* inadequacies."

Her words hit me like a blast of concrete to the chest. I stop dancing, releasing her abruptly.

Bid on her *virginity*?

That's what's going on here this weekend? Oh, hell no. Not on my watch.

My shock distracts me momentarily from the approaching guards. Before I can reply, they're upon us.

"Time to go, Paloma." The asshole who was making her eat last night takes her elbow.

"She's not going anywhere," I snarl before I remember to hide my aggression.

Paloma disengages from me, though. "Watch it. I'm not your property yet."

Thom drops a hand on my shoulder. "Looks like my daughter doesn't care to dance, Darius."

I grind my teeth as the guards hustle her away, not just out of my grasp but out of the room. The concrete that hit my chest has traveled down to my gut now. I want to pummel Thom to a pulp. My bear wants to rampage, but I contain myself.

I've spent the last fifteen years learning to control my impulses.

Every action must be well-thought out when you live among vultures. Especially when you're not the same species as them.

I won't win a hand-to-hand fight against the nearly forty security guards I've clocked around the premises. I need to bide my time, find where they took Paloma, and bust her out of the horror that appears to be her life.

I force myself to turn and give Thom a bland smile. "Fantastic party. Too bad your security team keeps making a spectacle."

"I suppose I am overprotective of the ones in my care. It's my biggest flaw." He drops his tone like he's confiding in me. I need to get away from him before I punch his throat. Paloma's scent is fading, and my bear is urging me to follow her before I lose the trail. But then he says something that makes me and my bear focus. "Paloma is...not well."

"I'm sorry to hear that." That might explain the bitter quality to her scent. A medicine perhaps? "Can anything be done?"

"Already handled, my boy. It's nothing the doctors can't deal with." He pats my shoulder again, looking past me. "Ah, I see I'm needed elsewhere."

At the opposite end of the room, a bunch of geriatric billionaires are exiting the ballroom, along with their sons. Thom walks to join them.

I fall into step beside him. "Is there a meeting?"

"Just a bit of personal business. Nothing for you to concern yourself with." He waves a hand, and two burly bodyguards block my way. "Enjoy the party." He leaves the room with his friends.

I step forward but stop when the guards don't move. "Private party?" I ask, pointing. The last remaining Chinless Chad gets roped by his father and disappears behind closed double doors.

"Invite only. You're not invited."

I could crack these goons' heads together and chase

down Thom, but I don't need to. I already know what's happening behind those closed doors. The auction. Thom's selling off his foster daughter like she's a medieval princess.

I hope the bidding takes a long time. I'll need it to get to Paloma.

I shrug like the bodyguards have won and drift back across the ballroom in the direction that the security team took Paloma. I clock a few more thugs in suits standing at that exit, barring the way. Two of them glare at me, and I resist the urge to give them a cheeky salute.

I grab another glass of champagne and sip it. A few models stand around in a circle, looking bored, and I saunter over to them.

"You ladies ever been here before?"

Two of them shake their heads.

"Would you like a tour?"

Ten minutes later, I traipse around the garden with a group of giggling party-goers. A bunch of normal guests followed me and the models. Everyone's a bit more raucous than usual, probably because I invited them to take shots before we went on the 'tour'.

"This way." I step up to a door that's near the west wing of the house and block everyone's view with my body, so I can break the lock. "The best paintings are in here." I lead the group inside.

"Is that a Picasso?" a few people cluster around a cubist painting of a woman.

"Indeed," I say. "It's probably worth close to one hundred million dollars."

Since there's no sign or scent of Paloma, I stay near the door as the others crowd in.

I catch her scent.

Go, my bear urges. I clamp down on my urge to go roaring down the hall.

"Are you on something?" A model close to me frowns, peering at my face. "Your eyes are...weird."

"Jaundice," I tell her, and she looks at me askance. She's too smart to buy my lie. I wink to make her think it's all a joke. "I've got eye drops in my room. I'll be right back. I think there's a Monet further down and around the corner," I toss over my shoulder as I walk out, prompting squeals of delight.

I follow Paloma's scent down the corridor. I'm trailed by a dozen party-goers who still see me as their pied piper.

"Hey! What are you doing in here?" a guard shouts as we round a corner. He's caught the back of the group. "You're not supposed to be back here." I'm out of sight, but from the sound of it, he and the other guards are trying to herd guests back to the ballroom. The entitled, inebriated guests turn belligerent, talking back, leaving me free to continue my search.

I follow Paloma's fresh scent down the hall. I'm deep in the west wing now. I haven't seen any guards, but I can hear them murmuring to each other somewhere up ahead.

I stride, full steam ahead, and pass a door that smells wrong. I stop and turn the handle. Inside is a small, dark room that looks like a medical examination room at a doctor's office. There's an exam table and no other furniture besides a white wall cabinet and freezer unit with a glass door.

This is where the medicinal smell is coming from. Thom told me Paloma wasn't well but hinted that she has the best medical care money can buy. Her illness has to be serious if there's a room dedicated to a doctor's visit here.

I take a moment to search the cabinet drawers. Boxes of

medical gloves and syringes–everything a doctor or nurse would need to administer a dose of medicine.

The freezer is the sort pharmacists use to keep vaccines at a certain temperature. It holds shelves and shelves of vials filled with blue liquid.

Poison, my bear warns, but that makes sense. Human medicine would smell like poison to an animal. I force myself to open the door and take a sniff, to see if I can detect anything specific. The smell is razor sharp, like tiny blades cutting my nasal passages. Up close, even a human would be able to smell it. I know humans use harsh compounds to save lives–like chemo to target cancer cells–but this smells so wrong.

The sense of urgency to get to Paloma grows. Time is ticking away.

Right now the auction Thom's running is the perfect distraction. I need to find her before the window of opportunity closes.

I shut the door, and move along. Paloma's scent still hovers on the air, a siren call to me and my bear. I force myself to pace slowly, keeping an eye out for guards.

Her sweet floral scent grows stronger, and I know I'm close. Then I hear her voice.

"No," she's telling someone. "I want to stay in my room."

I've reached the last corner. The hall ends twenty feet from where I stand. Paloma and a group of guards are arguing in front of a huge, round doorway.

These guys aren't in suits like the bodyguards, but black military-like uniforms. Thom has a private army guarding his precious Paloma. Several of them are packing some serious heat.

"I'll help you." The biggest guard goes to take her arm.

My eyes flare bright, and I have to fight to keep my bear from erupting.

"I can handle it," Paloma snaps, and the man drops his hand. The movement saves his life. I'd have killed him if he touched her. "I can walk. Just leave me alone."

"Go then." The head guard–the one who tried force-feeding her last night–steps aside and Paloma disappears. The huge door swings shut behind her. It's round, like the door to a bank vault. There's a jarring snap when all the locks engage.

Looks like they locked Paloma in tight for the night.

The head guard orders his men to fan out. Some of them head out for patrol, but most of them stay with their backs to the door.

I could run and take most of them out in a surprise attack, but then I'd waste time breaking into that vault door. Plus, I'd alert the entire manse and there are at least thirty-five other guards roaming this property.

I need another way in.

I stroll back the way I came, and out into the garden again. Paloma's room is at the far end of the west wing, in a literal stone tower. She's locked away like a princess.

Guards patrol the perimeter, but they're facing outward, as if expecting an attack from the road.

There's plenty of footholds in the stone, and a bunch of ivy I can grip if I need. Werebears are great at climbing.

I wait until clouds drift over the moon and begin my ascent.

* * *

Paloma

Moonlight streams into my room. The window creaks

42

and strands of ivy dance in the wind. I stand and look out at the night sky. I'd give anything to be able to open the window to the ocean breeze. I smack my hand against the shatter-proof glass in frustration, then plop on my bed, facing the night sky.

I've changed into a pink sleep set, so I can relax. My book's on the nightstand, but I'm too on edge to settle in and finish it.

At least I'm alone. I used to hate being locked in my room, but now it's a welcome reprieve. It's my final night of freedom.

I rub my right arm. My biceps is sore from tonight's injection. I'm woozy from my medicine.

A few years ago, after a normal check up and flu shot, I got so dizzy I had to lie down. Thom has hired doctors from every corner of the earth. They still don't know what's wrong, but narrowed it down to some sort of auto-immune disease. Thom restricts my internet access, so I can't do any research on my own, but the cocktail of meds they inject me with every few days keeps the symptoms at bay.

On my most successful escape attempt, I got off the property, only to collapse within twenty-four hours. Extreme weakness is a side effect of the disease. I'll need regular injections for the rest of my life to stay mobile. If I don't get them, the weakness will spread until my organs shut down.

I'm grateful that the disease responds to treatment. But now Thom has several ways to keep me tethered to this life: my sister and the medicine that keeps me alive.

And he intends to breed me. He'll make my children chattel, just like he did me. I'll never stop fighting, but I have no idea what to do. Hope is a faint light, disappearing over the horizon.

My head is fuzzy from the medicine, but the churning in my stomach is about the auction.

The window creaks again. The frame shudders and then the shatter-proof glass does the impossible. It cracks, bows inward, and explodes into a million glinting shards.

I'm frozen, unable to react. My thoughts move slowly like I'm underwater, and I can only watch as a dark shape fills the empty space. The intruder pauses a moment before jumping lightly to the floor and standing up straight. The low light gilds his wild blond hair.

"Hello, Rapunzel."

Chapter Four

Paloma

Paloma

It's the Viking. Here. In my room. He just climbed the tower and broke the window, and now he flashes a grin like this is normal.

My mouth hangs open. Electricity buzzes over my skin at the sight of him, and my heart starts pumping.

I force my heavy limbs to move and scramble off the bed, putting my four-poster between me and him. Another wave of wooziness washes over me. I'm out of breath like I've been running, but I finally find my voice. "What are you doing?" I grab the first thing at hand–my thick paperback–and heave it at him. My arm feels floppy.

It's not a great throw, but he catches the book and turns it over to examine the cover. "I've heard of this author. Is she any good?"

"Get out." I point to the window.

He strolls forward and places the book on my bed. The movement draws attention to his powerful shoulders. My room feels smaller with him here.

He holds up his hands. "I mean you no harm."

"I know that." I say it before I realize it's true. I feel safe with him. There's a magnetism between us. He's interested in me the same way I'm interested in him. In the old-fashioned, boy-likes-girl kind of way. Not just the I-want-you-because-you'll-make-me-billions-of-dollars way although I'm sure he wants that, too.

He paces around the bed, coming closer. I have nowhere to back up, but I'm fixed where I stand, fascinated by his fluid movements.

A few paces away, he stops. "You're not afraid of me."

"No," I agree. "But you shouldn't be here." I still haven't screamed for help. I don't know why not. A part of me doesn't want to watch as my guards invade my private space and tear him apart.

A part of me wants to savor this moment. He's huge and handsome, and my body remembers how gently he held me when we danced. The charm of his smile.

The cold night air invades my bedroom, sending goosebumps prickling on my skin. I'm extra aware of how little I'm wearing. Thin silk covers my breasts and bare sex and does nothing to hide my pert nipples.

To his credit, the Viking keeps his eyes on my face. "Let's go, Rapunzel." He holds his huge ham-hand out to me.

I flick a glance at it then find myself staring. What could a big man like that do with those hands on my body?

Wow–why am I thinking that?

Oh yeah,–because tonight's my virgin auction, and this guy decided to skip to the front of the line and take me without paying.

I really should scream. But Thom would kill him. Now that I'm sure he killed my parents, I know these guards aren't for show. Who knows how many deaths they've orchestrated on Thom's behalf? And for some reason, even though the man in my bedroom must be equally despicable, I don't want him to die. I'm fascinated by him.

I edge back. "You need to leave. It's not safe."

"*You're* not safe. That's why I'm here, princess." He takes a step forward and beckons to me. His eyes have a strange sheen to them, bright and honey-colored like a summer moon. "Chinless Chad is bidding on you right now. Let's get out of here before he or some other limp dick is declared the winner."

"Because your dick isn't limp?" I fold my arms over my chest and arch a brow, but a flush crawls up my neck as I find myself actually considering that part of his anatomy.

Okay, fine–I look.

There's a bulge in his pants that tells me limp-dick syndrome is *not* a problem for this guy. Um, yeah. *Not at all.*

I try and fail to swallow as I think again about what it would be like for this behemoth of a man to take my virginity.

Heat blooms on my skin and rolls up from my belly to my chest. I refuse to believe I'm reacting to him. It must be the medicine giving me a hot flash.

The Viking tilts his head as if he hears something outside the door although I hear nothing. "Come on, Paloma." He beckons again, losing the casual air of seduction. There's an urgency to his tone now. "We need to go. Now."

The room spins a little from the medication. I'm not steady on my feet.

Some reckless part of me wants to go with him. But I can't run away again–Thom will take it out on Wren.

I shake my head. "I can't go with you. If you want me, go put your bid in with the others."

I would very much prefer he win the bid. But he obviously doesn't have the bank roll for that, or he wouldn't have scaled the wall outside to break into my room.

He turns his head again, listening to something I can't hear. "Okay, princess. Sorry about this." He closes the distance between us, leans over, and puts his shoulder in the crease of my hip and straightens, effectively lifting me like a sack of potatoes over his back. "We'll have to do things my way."

My stomach flip-flops as the world turns upside down. I grab at his pants, but all I manage to do is feel up his iron hard hamstrings and glutes. "Stop!" I whisper-shout. My choice has already been made—I'm not going to get him killed by raising my voice.

But I should. Because he might get *me* killed if he leaves without my medication. Or get Wren killed if Thom thinks I'm part of this.

"I can't...you can't... Stop!"

But it's too late. The Viking somehow manages to climb out the window *with me over his shoulder*—an impossible feat—and starts to scale the wall. He has to release me to catch hold of the vines with both hands, and I teeter over his shoulder.

"Eep!" My arms aren't working properly, but I do my best to cling to his waist to keep from plummeting and breaking my neck. "I'm too heavy for you to carry. Are you trying to kill me?" I'm still whisper-shouting.

But I'm not going to die because the Viking moves so swiftly, we're already close to the ground. He doesn't make me feel heavy, either. He makes it seem like I'm as light as a feather.

"No, sweetheart. I'm trying to save you."

My head is full of cotton balls, but I try to work out his words.

Save me. The Viking is here to save me. That's a great romance novel twist.

We hit the ground, but he doesn't put me down; he sprints across the lawn with me still on his shoulder.

The noise and activity of party-goers must protect us from the guards' notice because the Viking makes it all the way to the giant circle drive before we're spotted.

"Hold it right there!" One of them booms. In his earpiece, he shouts, "The asset has been lifted. Repeat, the asset has been lifted!"

Shouts sound all around us.

The Viking pauses for a moment, turning and taking it all in before he sprints faster than should be humanly possible into the woods.

"Help!" I call out, not because I want to be saved, but to be sure Thom doesn't think I'm complicit in this. I don't want Wren's life to be in danger because of whatever foolish plan

Someone fires a shot. From the stables, Starlight whinnies, as if she knows I'm in danger.

I hear another voice yell, "Weapons tight! Weapons tight! Do not harm the asset."

Being described as an asset makes me want to puke.

No, actually, it's the hanging upside down over the massive shoulder of a guy dodging through the dark trees. That plus the medicine that's still making me feel sick.

I guess my kidnapper really is a Viking, right down to the raiding and plundering. Too bad he's going to get us both killed.

I pound his back. "This isn't going to save me!"

* * *

Darius

Paloma is scared.

I can tell because her scent changed to metallic fear when shots were fired. I almost shifted because my bear wanted to tear every last asshole to pieces. Before that, I could have sworn I detected the faint honeyed scent of her arousal, as if some part of her liked being carried off over my shoulder.

Now she's freaking out, and I want to kill the mother-fucker who fired his weapon. I'm pretty sure he shot into the air to alert the others because what idiot would fire in the dark at 'the asset'? Either way, I'm almost tempted to let my bear out to tear him limb from limb. But there's no time to go on a rampage, and I don't trust my bear not to hurt Paloma while he's at it.

I need to get Paloma out of here and soothe her.

Preferably with her clothes off.

Oops. Scratch that entirely inappropriate thought.

It's just that she's wearing the most delectable satin shorts and cami with absolutely nothing else on, and I have the insane idea that I want to mark her right now to keep all these other fuckers off her.

Not that humans would recognize my claim on her.

And I *do* want to lay my claim on her.

"Put me down!" Paloma beats on my back with her fists.

"Hold on. I'm going to get you out of here," I tell her. I dash through the dark forest. The sky overhead is overcast, and I take advantage of the darkness to cut across Thom's estate to find the road. We've outpaced the guards, for now.

I burst out of the trees onto the road. The roar of an engine tells me a car is coming.

Perfect.

A black Lamborghini roars up to us. I can tell by the

way the car hugs the shoulder of the road that the driver is inebriated. It's one of Thompson's guests exiting the property, not a guard.

The driver doesn't see me in time to stop, but I throw a leg out and stop it with my foot in the grill. The back tires skid to the side. The grill folds and dents around my foot.

Paloma kicks her legs. I still don't set her down, not until I reach the passenger's door, throw it open, and hold out my hand for the passenger inside–one of the plastic models from the party.

"Are you okay?" the drunk driver asks. He's in a tux, still wearing his mask, which sits askew on his face. A white dust of cocaine around his nose and his date's remind me that they were part of my tour group.

"Oh, it's you!" the model giggles. She takes my hand, and I help her out of the car, then gently settle Paloma in her stead.

"What are you doing, man?" the douchebag in the driver seat demands.

"Get out. It's an emergency. She needs medical attention," I clip.

It's not really a lie. Her reactions are slowed, I presume from the medication they gave her. Otherwise, I think she would be harder to manage.

"What? Oh, damn." The driver's reactions are slower than Paloma's.

I've already fastened Paloma's seatbelt and shut her door.

I jog around the car, throw open the driver's side door, and pull the guy out of the car. He forgot to wear a seatbelt.

His bad.

I toss him to the side and jump behind the wheel before

51

Paloma can get her door open. She's fumbling for it, but her reactions are slow.

I slam my foot down on the gas pedal, and we shoot forward, accelerating from zero to ninety in about three seconds.

Damn. This is fun. I keep my foot pressed down, watching the speedometer climb to one hundred. One-ten. One hundred and fifteen miles per hour.

I definitely picked the right car to steal.

Paloma's hand is still on the door handle, like she's considering whether she can open the door and jump out.

"Careful, princess. We're going way too fast to survive a jump," I warn.

She looks over her shoulder behind us at the black SUVs just now pulling out of the drive. "Yes, I see that. But they're going to find us, you know."

"Not if I can help it."

I fish my phone out of my pocket and dial the number of a wolf shifter I know. Not Brick Blackthroat, the alpha who I box with at the gym, but his enforcer, Sully.

"Sully, hey," I say when he answers. "Darius Medvedev. The, ah–" I'm trying to think of a code word for *bear,* but he cuts me off.

"Yeah, of course. I know who you are. What's up?"

"I need a safe house–out of the city. Can you hook me up?"

"Yeah. Where are you now?"

"Hamptons."

"Roger that. You have transpo? Is Rhode Island too far?"

I let out a breath. "That's perfect."

"Texting a location."

"Great. Thank you."

"You need protection?"

"No, I got it."

"Care to tell me what's going on? I know your kind like to go solo, but–"

"I'm good." Wolves. Their *pack or die* thing is just way too much. "I'll be in touch if I do need an assist. I appreciate the offer."

"Yep." Sully ends the call without further niceties. I appreciate a guy who values efficiency over bullshit.

Paloma stares at me with wide, brown eyes. "*Safe-house?*" she demands. "Who *are* you?"

I flash her a grin. "Darius Medvedev, at your service."

"Service? Is that what you call snatching me from my bedroom in the middle of the night?" She looks down at her miniscule satin PJs. "With no clothes?"

I don't mean to, but I glance at her incredible, full breasts shifting beneath the thin pink satin of her cami. The corners of my lips kick up. "I fail to see that particular aspect of our adventure as a problem."

"Oh is that what you're calling this?"

"I had to get you out of there."

She looks back over her shoulder, but I'm driving over a hundred miles an hour. The headlights from the SUVs behind us grow smaller and smaller. "You have to take me back."

"Not happening, princess."

"You don't understand. Thom is not a nice man. He will kill you. He'll kill us both if he thinks I'm a part of this. "

"Yeah, I gathered. He had you *locked in your room* like a prisoner. Men were *bidding on your virginity* tonight." I know my eyes are glowing again because I can feel my bear clawing to get out. He wants to dismember every man who thought to deflower her.

She alternates staring at me and looking back at the pursuing vehicles.

"Also, how can a woman as beautiful as you still be a virgin?" I give my head a hard shake. "Nevermind–I know. Because you've been locked in that tower your whole life."

I try again not to look and fail. Her nipples have hardened to stiff points under the flimsy fabric. Even in the darkness, I can see a flush of color travel up her neck and spread across her gorgeous cleavage.

"You didn't know about the breeding part until I told you at the ball, did you?"

My bear nearly erupts to the surface then. I don't know whether it's from anger at the idea of her being bred or a base animal interest in breeding her myself. Before I can stop it, a low growl emits from my chest.

"No," my bear snarls before I have him on leash. I need to get control of him before I do something even more reckless than stealing a fair maiden from her tower high. What is it about this woman that makes me nearly come unhinged?

"Is that why you crawled through my window to save me?"

"I was already trying to piece together why Thompson had you under constant guard. But yes, that was enough reason to risk my standing in Thompson's world to get you out of there."

She considers me. "I thought you were there to bid on me, too."

"I gathered."

"I thought you might be Thom's idea of a perfect stud."

"Why?"

"Oh, I don't know because you're twice the size of the other men and can swim in a cold ocean with your shirt off?"

54

My lips twitch. "Did you think I should've swum in my tux?"

"Shut up."

"Did that impress you, Rapunzel?"

"Definitely not." Her inner thighs clamp together, and the sweet perfume of her arousal fills the small cabin of the car.

Yep, she was impressed.

The admiration is mutual.

"I just thought Thom picked you because you're a perfect" –she flaps her hand at me– "*specimen* or something."

"I swear I knew nothing about the auction, Paloma."

"So you're not part of the evil scheme. In that case..." She looks out the window, and I get the sense it's to hide her face. The scent of her arousal blooms stronger.

My cock stirs in response. Just beneath the surface, my bear rumbles, rattling his cage.

Let me out.

My blood is running south of my waist. I prompt, "In that case?"

"In that case..." She cranes her neck to look behind us. We're well away from danger now, zipping at more than twice the speed of the other cars. In a few miles, I'll change highways toward Rhode Island. She turns back and looks me over, thoughtfully. "Giving you my virginity would be the perfect way to sabotage Thom's grand plans for me."

Chapter Five

Paloma

Darius makes a strange growling sound and steps on the accelerator. I thought we were going fast before, but now he's actually flooring it. I hang onto the door handle of the sports car he "borrowed" and glance at the speedometer. One hundred and fifteen miles an hour.

Is he racing to get me to a bed?

My heart speeds along with the car.

This is really happening. The Viking is going to bed me.

Pluck my flower.

Breed me.

I know–I've definitely read way too many historical romance novels. Still, the horror of Thom's plan becomes way more palatable when my Viking is the stud in question. Maybe this is just my way of taking back control in the only limited way I have. Making sure that there's no virginity left to auction when Thom gets to me gives me satisfaction.

But it's not just that.

I'm twenty-four years old. I've been imprisoned for the last ten years of my life, with no television and limited internet access. Riding Starlight and reading romance novels have been my only pleasures. And yes, those novels may have inspired a healthy interest in sex.

I want to know what it would be like to be claimed by this marauding Viking.

I want to guide his pulsing member into my quivering quim, or whatever the words are. I want it.

With him.

And judging by the tent in his tuxedo pants, he wants it, too.

We whiz past a sign, and he hits the brakes, then takes a turn at a speed that makes the tires screech.

My body pitches against the door, and I hang onto the handle. I would be alarmed, but he handles himself with such surety, such efficiency, that I'm confident he knows what he's doing. I feel strangely safe with him, despite the fact that he's put me and Wren in terrible danger.

I'll just go with him for the night. I'll deflower myself with his giant Viking cock and then escape back to Thom.

That's the only way to make sure Wren stays safe.

Besides, I'll need my medicine within forty-eight hours, or I could die.

The dark trees whip by my window. I twist to look over my shoulder, but Thom's men are far behind. We may actually get away.

Speeding away from Lockepoint, I feel safer than I have in the ten years since my parents died.

–Were *killed*.

But just because I'm momentarily free of Thom and his dastardly schemes doesn't mean the nightmare is over.

Still, it's a momentary reprieve.

With an extremely hot Viking who literally carried me

off over his shoulder. It was remarkably similar to the fantasy I had of him carrying me off to the beach.

It's both exhilarating and terrifying to leave Thom's property. I haven't been off that plot of land since I tried to escape five years ago. That time, I broke into someone's summer house down the road. I knew the neighbors never used their vacation homes. I holed up there overnight, trying to get through to Wren at her boarding school, but the nuns wouldn't let me speak with her.

That was before I knew how dependent I was on the medicine. I passed out the next morning. Thom's guards found me that afternoon and brought me back to Locke-point. The doctor said I nearly died.

"While I absolutely *love* that taking your virginity is on the table, that's not why I claimed you. Er–grabbed you. Whatever." His eyes glow with some strange trick of the light.

God, he's gorgeous. His hair seems longer than it did last night, almost like it grew to fit my fantasy. Being in this small space with him is doing crazy things to my body. There's a slow thrum between my legs that grows more insistent with each moment.

"I sort of prefer the term *claim*."

His brows pop, and he chokes a little. "What?"

"Yeah, it goes with your marauding Viking vibe."

His lips twitch. "My what?"

"Listen–this is my fantasy. I get to control the narrative of my deflowering."

"Absolutely." The word rockets out of his mouth. "Absolutely, you do." His cock is thick and fat along one leg. I'm tempted to reach out and touch it through his pants.

"I will" –he clears his throat– "be your marauding

Viking, if that's how you want me. But, like I said, that's not what this was about."

All I can think about is sex—what it will be like with Darius. Will he be on top? Take me from behind? Or should I control the whole scene and straddle his waist for my very first time?

But his words finally sink in. "What is this about, then?" But as soon as I say it, I realize I don't want to know.

I managed to get away from Lockepoint, at least for the night.

I'm going to have sex for the first time with this beautiful stranger.

I don't want to think about all the rest of the ugliness of my ugly life. I reach out and put my fingers on his luscious lips. "No wait." I stop him from speaking. "Don't tell me. Can I just have this fantasy? Just for tonight?"

He parts his lips, and I feel the golden stubble around them as he takes my fingertips into his mouth and sucks.

Fingers aren't erotic. At least, I wouldn't have thought they were. But I feel an answering tug between my legs, as if my fingertips and quim are linked.

A soft moan comes from my lips. My sex gets slick. I wish I had panties on because I fear my arousal will get all over the seat of the car.

"You want me to play Viking for you tonight?" Darius' voice is rough.

When I take my hand away, he catches my wrist and holds it.

"Is this the medication talking?" He tugs my fingers back to his mouth and nibbles on my knuckles.

"No! Definitely not. This is me controlling my own destiny. I get to choose who I give my virginity to, and I choose you."

He takes my index finger into his mouth and sucks, his tongue swirling around it.

I cry out. My nipples are hard points, my breasts feel heavy. My God–I might come from finger-sucking alone.

"You choose *me* to take your virginity?" His voice is an octave lower than before, which seems impossible since he was already a baritone. Something about the light in the car makes his eyes look golden. "A guy you don't even know?"

He seems to be at war with himself because at the same time he argues with me, he slides my hand down his muscled body until it reaches the tree trunk that makes up his thigh. From there, I know where he's headed. It's where I wanted to go. I slide my palm over the thick outline of his cock, marveling at how hard and long it is.

"I choose the Viking." My voice is husky. "That's you for tonight."

"Ah." I feel his belly shudder in and out as I stroke my fingers slowly up his length. "I see." His breath is ragged.

I remove my hand and sit back. "But if you're not willing..." For the first time, ever, I have a sense of a woman's power over a man.

This is the reason men like Thom hold women captive or force them to breed. They're working so hard to master something that frightens them. That could control them if they're not careful.

He catches my wrist again and pulls it to his mouth. This time, he parts his lips and moves them across my pulse, inhaling deeply like my scent has some erotic power over him. Which is strange because I'm not wearing any perfume. Why would the girl in the tower need to smell good?

"I'm willing, princess. I'll be your Viking. I'll be whatever you want me to be tonight. Like you said, it's your fantasy. Who am I to deny a woman her deepest desires?"

A tiny orgasm ripples through me at that. My ass lifts off the seat, and my thighs slap together as the muscles grip and spasm.

The Viking looks over. "Did you just come?"

I'm breathless. This fantasy is fantastic. "Yes."

He shakes his head slowly and tsks, all the while still driving twice the speed limit and passing the few cars that are out on this highway tonight. "Naughty princess. You're the Viking's prize. Don't you know?" His eyes gleam in the headlights of an oncoming car. "You don't get to come without permission."

The flesh between my legs lifts and tightens.

"If you do it again, I'll have to take you across my knees for a real Viking punishment."

* * *

Darius

I'm about to come in my pants, too.

Let me out.

My bear claws to free himself.

My dick is harder than stone. I should pay more attention to the road and keep a lookout for law enforcement, since I'm driving a stolen car at one hundred over the posted limit, but Paloma just said she wanted me to *claim* her.

I know she has no idea what that means to me, but my bear heard what he heard.

And he is *more* than on board.

Fuck. I have to be careful. My bear is wild. Totally uncivilized. Savage.

If he gets control while I'm touching Paloma–if he tries

to permanently mark and claim her as ours–she could be in real danger. Not that he would mean to hurt her, but she's a fragile human. He's a feral beast. If he tried to mark her, she could die.

I can't let him free near her. Not ever.

Paloma moans at my words. I need to get control of this situation.

"Here's what I want you to do, princess." I use my boardroom voice–the one that makes my employees jump to please me.

"Lean that seat back."

She obeys, fumbling with the buttons on the side of her seat until she finds the right one.

"Good girl."

"Now, put your fingers between your legs and close your eyes. Get that pussy nice and wet for me while you think about what your Viking is going to do when he gets you to his keep. Understand?"

Her fingers slide into her satin pajama shorts, and she lays her head back on the reclined seat. "She's going in protest," she warns me as she closes her eyes.

"Then I'll have to force her to obey. How does she like to be forced?"

"She likes to be carried off over his big brawny shoulder. Maybe she needs to be tied up–loosely, of course. And..." – her voice waivers a little– "maybe that other thing you mentioned."

I hide a smile. "A good, hard spanking, over my knee?"

"Maybe not that hard," she says in a small voice.

I chuckle. "She's going to have the night of her dreams."

Paloma follows my instructions, keeping her eyes closed and her fingers moving between her legs. But eventually, as I hoped, she slides into slumber.

Thank fuck. It's at least another three hours to the safe house, and my dick was going to explode if we kept up the foreplay.

I speed through Connecticut, keeping an eye out for highway patrol. As I drive, the insanity of my actions sink in.

I let my bear instinct rule when I snatched Paloma from Thompson's claws.

I'm not sorry—not even remotely. Just having her beside me in the car brings out a wild exhilaration. But I realize there will be drastic consequences. Thompson is a powerful man.

I just picked a war with an eccentric evil billionaire who clearly has no moral compass. Unlike Thompson, I'm not well-connected. I don't have cronies in every high office whose pockets I've lined to be sure they'll lie, steal, and cheat for me.

I'm a newcomer to Wall Street. I wasn't born into wealth—I made it from nothing. And I only recently got my company to nine figures. I don't even have the power of a pack behind me like Brick Blackthroat and the werewolves of Wall Street.

I come from a small, rag-tag adoptive family in the rural mountains of New Mexico. Sure, I can call on my brothers back home for protection or fire power, but if anything happened to one of them, it would break our mother's heart. And I've already broken her heart enough.

My feral bear and his wild rampages in my adolescence wore her out so much that she went into hibernation. My own twin brother won't speak to me over it.

I could keep it local and call on Brick Blackthroat and his wolf pack to help, but it's a lot to ask, and he has no obligation to give me his support. They just had a terrible internal conflict over Brick choosing a human as his luna, and they lost hundreds of members due to the infighting.

Either way, if I can't prevail against Thompson, this could end not only with my own financial and professional ruin, but, as Paloma has warned, in both of our deaths.

I can't even think beyond the immediate dilemma of keeping Paloma safe. My bear wants to claim her. Even if she were willing, I can't mate a human. My bear is way too volatile. Human females are far too fragile.

No.

I'll just have to figure out how to free Paloma from her evil foster father and then let her go.

My bear snarls—not a snarl echo beneath the surface, but an actual ferocious roar that comes out of my mouth and rattles the car.

Paloma startles awake, sitting forward and sucking in a gasp. "What was *that*?"

Chapter Six

P aloma

I wake in bed with my Viking.

I fell back to sleep after the loud motorcycle woke me up on the road. Darius told me we were almost there, and he'd wake me when we arrived, but I guess he's a liar. He must've carried me inside without me waking, which is crazy. Either the medicine made me extra drowsy, or I trust this guy completely. Plus, I'm heavy–as Thom always points out.

I sit up now and look around. I'm under the covers, but Darius lies on top of them, still fully dressed, as if he fell asleep while on guard. The 'safehouse' is not the barricaded basement bunker I imagined. Instead, it's a luxurious beach house. Light streams in through the windows of the bedroom we're in, which look out on the ocean.

I slip out from under the covers, careful not to wake Darius, and investigate. I discover we're in a gorgeous three-bedroom luxury vacation home. I use one of the bathrooms and wash my face. In a basket under the sink, I find the emergency toiletries one might need–unopened travel toothbrushes and toothpastes, mini bottles of mouth-wash, individually wrapped combs. Even sunscreen and lip balm. I brush my teeth, comb my hair, and put on some lip balm.

Then I investigate the kitchen. The cupboards are stocked with canned goods. We won't starve here.

There's a fancy Nespresso machine that takes me a while to figure out, but when I do, produces an incredible cup of coffee. I open a shelf-stable box of whipping cream to pour in and turn it blond.

"Paloma?" Darius calls from the bedroom, a sharp note of panic in his voice.

"I'm in here," I call back. I put a second pod in the machine and set a mug underneath to make him a cup.

He emerges from the bedroom. He's in his bare feet, but still wearing his rumpled tuxedo shirt and pants from last night. The bowtie is gone, and the black shirt is open at the throat, revealing a patch of golden curls above the neckline of his undershirt.

He rubs his jaw. I swear to God, he went from a closely shorn beard last night to almost full-on beard and mustache today, and his hair seems to be longer, too. But that's impossible. I must be confused.

"I can't believe I didn't hear you get up."

I'd forgotten how deep his voice is. How much I enjoy the gravelly rumble of it.

"I'm sure you were tired. What time did we get here?"

"Close to five a.m. But I don't usually sleep heavily." His gaze at me is both sleepy and speculative. "I must trust you."

His words startle me. "That's weird," I mutter.

"What?"

"Just—I had the same thought when I woke up." I shove

my hair back from my face. "It's strange I didn't wake up when we got here."

"Mmm," he rumbles.

The Nespresso machine finishes, and I take the filled mug and hold it out to him. "Cream?"

"Thank you, princess." He reaches out, and I find myself marveling at how sexy the watch on his wrist looks. Not because it's some expensive designer piece–which it is– but because his wrist and forearm are things of beauty. The wide bone of his wrist is probably twice the diameter of mine, and the golden hair on his thick muscled forearm make the perfect backdrop to the Rolex, or whatever it is.

But then, everything about this giant is deeply attractive to me.

His fingers close around the mug, brushing mine. Flutters go off in my belly at the touch. "Yes, please, to the cream."

That rumbling voice! It stirs my insides even more.

I add cream from the little box to his mug while he watches me appreciatively.

There's no cunning or conniving in his gaze. It doesn't slice and dice me the way Thom's does. This man has a presence that seems to hold me. My body can relax around him, as if it knows I'm safe. I don't have to stay vigilant.

Which is false.

I'm *not* safe. And while I don't believe Darius would hurt me, we *are* in terrible danger.

Darius takes a sip of his coffee, watching me over the top of his mug.

The memory of the things he said to me last night come flooding back. *Good Girl. Get that pussy nice and wet for me while you think about what your Viking is going to do to you.*

Oh, Darius.

I can't stay here with him; nor can I let him get killed because of me. My best plan is to get out of here, away from him, and contact Thom. I can try to explain away Darius' behavior. He was drunk. Partying out on the lawn. He thought it would be funny to climb up and carry me off, and was too inebriated to understand that I didn't want him to take me.

Gah. Thom probably won't buy it. Maybe I'll make a deal on the phone with my foster father–I come back, and he leaves Wren and Darius alone.

Something like that.

All I know is that I have to get myself out of this beautiful, safe haven soon.

But before I do, I'm having hot, Viking sex. This may be my only chance to get something I want in life.

"Well, Viking?" I challenge him. "Is this your keep?"

His warm, steady gaze turns smoldering. His lips curve into a slow smile. "It is. For now." He doesn't take his eyes from mine.

"And what would you do if your princess tried to run?"

He doesn't move. He just takes another sip of coffee and watches me.

The anticipation of his reaction turns me into a live wire.

"There would be consequences, of course."

A tremor of excitement starts up behind my knees. The flesh between my legs lifts and squeezes. Without breaking eye contact, I slowly slide my coffee mug onto the counter.

Then, I take off running. I make it to the glass sliding doors and waste a few precious seconds figuring out how to get it unlocked. The glass on the doors seems extra-thick. Like maybe it's bullet-proof.

I throw the door open and realize Darius hasn't moved yet.

Is he going to chase me?

He'd better not ruin this for me.

"Run, princess." His murmur is a low rumble.

I take off sprinting across the deck and down the stairs to the sand below. I run for the water, where the wet sand will be better packed and easier to run on. Once there, I run as fast as I can.

It doesn't matter because when I look over my shoulder, Darius is right behind me, almost like he's holding back even after giving me a head start.

I shriek in surprise.

He lunges forward and catches me around my waist. "Bad princess," he murmurs in my ear as he spins me around. I cling to his muscled forearms. The gorgeous, corded tree trunks. "Now, I'm going to have to punish you." There's laughter in his voice.

My feet touch back onto the ground, and he slides his hand from my waist down between my legs. I gasp at the shock of contact. The firm touch of his fingers molding around my mons. At the same time, his other hand cups my breast, squeezing it. I lean my head back against his muscled chest as a riot of sensation rips through my body. His thumb rubs over my nipple. His fingers between my legs undulate with a rolling pressure.

Then, he throws me to my back, but I'm cradled so well in his strong arms that I feel nothing of a bump, I'm only surprised to find myself in the sand.

Just like my fantasy!

There's no slow seduction. He plays the part of the wild Viking perfectly. He yanks the satin crotch of my pajama shorts to the side and covers my entire pussy with his open mouth.

I cry out in shock and surprise. But mostly pleasure because his tongue is already moving there, delving between my folds. He penetrates me with his tongue, lashes me with it. He sucks on my lips. The hair of his overnight stubble create an added layer of sensation.

I'm lost. I'm in the throes of it immediately. My hands go to his hair—that thick golden mane—and I tug on it to urge him on.

Not that he requires urging.

The Viking knows what he's doing. His hand roams up beneath my cami to massage my breast and then pinch a nipple, all the while his masterful tongue teaches me that promised lesson for my disobedience.

It's a good one.

I arch up on the sand and moan my pleasure.

He pushes up on one hand to look down at my face as his fingers return to stroking my pussy. He presses one finger inside me—or at least he attempts to, but it's too thick. I noticed in the car that his digits are probably the size of a normal man's cock. He meets my natural resistance and eases back, then switches to a smaller finger—his pinky perhaps.

I'm out of breath with excitement.

He screws the finger inside me and pumps it slowly, all the while watching my face, perhaps for signs of discomfort. There is none.

Only pleasure.

I'm being ravished on the beach by a Viking. It's perfection.

He pumps a little faster, pinching my nipple roughly. Then he claims my mouth.

It's a savage kiss. His tongue sweeps into my mouth, and I taste my own essence on it.

My legs thrash around him on the sand. I wrap a hand behind his head to encourage more kissing, but he breaks it and lowers his mouth to my sex again. With his pinky still pumping in and out of me, he finds my clit with his tongue.

I shriek as pleasure explodes all around me. I come, my muscles squeezing around his finger, my back arching in the sand, my inner thighs shivering and shaking around his broad shoulders.

It doesn't last long enough, though. I still want more. I want the whole thing. I want his member between my legs.

When it passes and I open my eyes, Darius shakes his head with mock sternness. "That's the second time you've come without permission, princess."

I lie back in the sand, boneless and soaring from the experience.

The Vikings eyes glint amber in the sunlight.

"Now it's time for your punishment."

Darius

I stand and take Paloma's hand, drawing her straight from her back to my shoulder, so I can carry her like a war prize back to the castle.

My bear is riled up, which made it difficult to hold back once I had her taste on my tongue, but I didn't claim her.

I hope I wasn't too rough. Too un-nuanced. But if I was, it goes with the Viking fantasy.

As I carry her back to the safe house, with a taste of her still on my tongue, my bear roars in a victory dance. Nothing has ever felt so right as this moment. As claiming

Paloma. But no— I'm not going to *claim* her, I firmly remind myself and my bear.

I'm just going to fulfill her fantasy.

And what a fucking privilege. It's an honor I take extremely seriously.

And claim her, my bear insists.

No claiming. I slam the hatch down on him as I have a million times before. *Stay. In. You may not come out now. Not ever with Paloma.*

Claim. Her.

He is too soothed by her scent engulfing my head to put any teeth behind his demand.

I ignore him, thinking instead of all the wonderful dirty things I'm going to do to Paloma.

I brush the sand off the backs of her legs as I walk, and give her ass a light slap. She kicks her legs, but the scent of her arousal grows stronger.

"Princess, you belong to me now. That means your body belongs to me. Your orgasms belong to me. You will bend to my will or suffer the consequences."

I'm riffing on her Viking story. I don't know exactly what she has in mind, but I'm guessing it has to do with domination. Perhaps with not being held responsible for her sexual appetite. If she's tied up and forced, it can't be her fault. She'll still be a good girl. Perhaps these fantasies are the way her mind coped with her actual imprisonment. A way to reclaim the terror of having no control by making it sexy.

I need to get this right for her. I know she's turned on by the punishment idea—I can tell by the way her thighs squeeze together every time I mention it. I'll give her a light spanking and see how she reacts to it.

When I get back to the safe house, I use the keypad to

enter with the code that Sully texted me. The place is pimped out with every luxury a millionaire could desire. This is probably Blackthroat's version of roughing it. Paloma and I will have no trouble holding up here while I figure out how to get her completely free of her evil foster father.

I open the sliding glass door and step inside then tip my captive down in front of the sofa.

"Now, for your punishment." I whip the tiny spaghetti strap top off from over her head. I thought about ordering her to strip, but I'm assuming she doesn't want to voluntarily submit to me. She wants to be forced. She wants me to make it so she has no seeming choice in the matter.

"You were naughty this morning, princess." I hook my thumbs in the waistband of the silky shorts and yank them down below her ass, then give her round cheek one hard slap.

"Oh." She darts a look at me. Her eyes are wide, but her pupils are still dilated. There's no sign of fear.

I sit on the couch and tug her across my knees. Damn, if the scent of her honey doesn't grow even stronger. I lay my large palm on her ass, squeezing, but not moving it. Just letting her get used to the idea of her predicament. And always, waiting for her unspoken consent.

"I am the master of this keep," I tell her firmly. "And you will obey."

"I love that you know the word *keep*," Paloma mumbles an aside with amusement in her voice.

I can't stop the chuckle that rumbles in my chest, but I give her ass a slap to cover my break in character.

She moans softly. I tug her shorts down the rest of the way, so she can kick them off and spread her legs. When I slide my middle finger between her thighs, her honey is thick.

My cock presses painfully against the zipper of my tuxedo pants. "Looks like you did a good job of getting this pussy ready for me," I say.

"Mmm," she agrees.

"I'm still going to have to warm your ass. I mean *arse*. – Would it be arse?" I wonder aloud.

"Definitely *arse*," Paloma agrees with a breathy laugh.

I slap her ass a little harder this time. "You won't be laughing for long, my lady."

Her back tenses, so I rub a slow circle around her ass until the muscles relax again. I stroke between her legs with a long slow drag. "By the time I'm through, you'll be thoroughly ready to take my big Viking cock." I tuck the tip of my thick middle finger in her entrance, stretching her open.

She moans again, hollowing her lower back and lifting her ass in the air for more.

My middle finger slides in to the first knuckle. "Good girl," I praise.

"I thought I was a bad girl."

"Oh, you *do* want that spanking, don't you?"

I ease my finger out and give her what she needs, starting a steady rhythm of firm spanks that alternate right and left cheeks, concentrating them on the lower half of her ass where she sits.

"Oh! Ow!" One of her hands flies back to cover her ass, and I let her stop me. I rest my hand over hers and squeeze.

"Mmm," she moans wantonly.

"Are you going to run away again, Princess?" I'm thinking she's had enough of spanking, but she answers petulantly, "Yes."

I laugh, my fingers sliding between her legs again.

"Then I will have to give you a proper Viking fucking." My middle finger slides inside her more easily now. Her body's readying to take me. I'm able to get it into the second knuckle then all the way in.

Paloma moans.

I pump it inside her, then slip my finger out and spread the moisture to her clit. She wriggles over my lap, her reddened plump ass making an incredible spectacle.

Claim. Her.

My bear is crazy. He's been locked up for too long. Not only do I never let him out, but I haven't had sex with enough females in recent years. Now that I have a beautiful one naked and over my lap, he wants me to mark her.

I gather more moisture at her entrance with my fingertips and rub some of it over her back hole. She squeezes her cheeks together to keep me out. "A proper Viking fucking means you taking me in every hole." I give her right buttcheek a slap. "In your pussy–does a Viking say pussy?-- in your lady flower."

Paloma laughs. "My quim."

"Oh yes, that's what I want to fuck. This juicy pink quim." I stroke along her soaking slit in appreciation. Then I give her other cheek a slap. "Also this plump, perfect ass–I mean arse."

She squeezes her cheeks together again.

I don't really have any intention of taking her anal virginity this morning, too, but I'm improvising, and that's what came out, so I run with it.

"What's the third hole?" she asks.

I give her another spank. "So innocent, my lovely dove. Your mouth." I spank her again, several times, thoroughly warming her skin to a rosy glow. Then I reward her for taking it with another caress between her legs. "Your mouth is the third hole. I might start there."

Again, I'm not serious. There's no way I would feed my cock into the mouth of a virgin who's been locked up in a tower and likely has never even kissed a man. It might terrify her.

I'm able to get my middle finger inside her easily now, and I pump it in and out, which seems to drive her wild. She moans and rocks her pelvis over my lap, making my stiff cock leak pre-cum on my boxers.

"Okay, princess." I pull my finger out and give her ass one last slap. "It's time for the Viking to have his way with you."

I stand, scooping and rolling her up into my arms. I carry her back to the bedroom where I had the pleasure of guarding her this morning.

I toss her in the center of the bed and pull my discarded bowtie from the pocket of my tuxedo pants.

Her dark locks fall across her shoulders. Her face is flushed, eyes glassy from her spanking. Those full lips look so damn kissable.

She scoots back on the bed like she means to run again. I can tell it's just for play, by the mischievous twist to her lips.

I tug both ends of the bow tie and make it snap. The moment she tries to bolt over the edge of the bed, I reach out and grab her ankle, dragging her back. "Where do you think you're going, my pretty dove?"

I catch her wrists and tie them together with my bow tie.

She studies me in that intelligent way she has. "How do you know my name means *dove*? Do you speak Spanish?"

I nod. "Not well. But I have a passing knowledge of a dozen languages."

Her brows pop.

"Viking is one of them." I wink.

She laughs, as I hoped she would. Obviously, I know it's Norse.

I unbutton my tuxedo shirt. It was already open at the throat and halfway untucked from my pants, rumpled from our quick escape and being slept in. Paloma sits up on the bed and watches.

She rubs her lips together when my undershirt comes off, eyeing my hairy chest. I unbutton the tuxedo pants and slide them off with my silk boxers. My cock springs out, standing at attention. Ready for action. It's been low-level throbbing ever since she touched it through my pants last night. Right now it's so hard, I fear it could break off.

Paloma's gaze drops to it, and while her eyes widen again, she doesn't seem daunted. Of course, she doesn't know what she doesn't know.

I climb on the bed and catch her bound wrists. I lift them over her head, then use them to slowly lever her onto her back. With her wrists pinned above her head, I hold her down and give her a long, slow kiss.

"Mmm." She squirms beneath me.

Her body is soft and lush. I adore her curves. That there's enough meat on her bones to fill my hands.

I cup her breast and squeeze. I lower my mouth to one of her nipples and roll my tongue over it, then suck hard. I let my teeth scrape the skin as I release and move to the other one.

Claim her.

My bear clamors for my attention, but I have none to

spare for his demands. It's Paloma's beautiful body that occupies all of my focus.

I travel south, pushing her knees up and spreading them wide, so I can lick into her soft sex. She's still dripping wet from her spanking and the taste of her honey nearly makes me shift into bear form right there.

No. I'm even more savage in keeping him down. I blink hard to change my eyes back to normal.

Not. Normal, my bear snarls.

I slam the door on his cage as I learned to do when I first moved to Manhattan. I suppress him, cram him into a tight little box way down below my belly where he can't get out.

I need to be able to focus on Paloma. She has a fantasy she wants fulfilled, and I intend to make it perfect for her.

I slide my tongue between her labia, tracing around her inner lips and swirling over her clit. It's work, but I manage to get my thumb inside her this time while I suck her clit.

She pants and struggles to accommodate me. I don't feel any resistance, though. No cherry to pop. She's just tight.

"You gonna take my big Viking cock, little dove?" Gone is the Wall Street hedge fund manager. He's been replaced by the rough, wild bear man from New Mexico. But I'm supposed to be a Viking, not a bear.

Never a bear. I can't regress to those days when my bear had more control than I did.

"No." Paloma shakes her head, and for a moment, I think she means it, but then I realize she's still playing the game where I hold her down and make her take it. Where I force her to do something the innocent maiden would never do of her own volition.

I can tell because she overacts. She shakes her head violently and pushes back at me with her bound wrists at the same time her knees try to drive me forward.

"Your safe word is *Bad bear*," I tell her before I have a chance to censor my words. I never give out any personal details about myself. Especially not the name of the mountain where I come from or the animal that is my true nature.

But Paloma's different.

Mate, my bear insists.

She gives me a quick nod, confirming my belief that it wasn't a real no.

I push her knees wider to kneel between them and grab a pillow to shove under her hips.

"This is so I can take you deep and hard," I warn her.

"I'll never submit!" she cries, like the captured princess she pretends to be.

I arch a stern brow. "Oh, you'll submit, my lovely stolen bride. You'll submit every night until I fill your womb with my giant Viking baby."

Paloma laughs breathily. The weight of her tits makes them fall open to the sides. I want to worship her body for the rest of my life.

I lightly slap the side of one of her breasts—not enough to hurt, just enough to surprise her. Her eyes fly to my face and stay glued there, as if she's watching me to see what I will do next.

I review my words, and realize I don't actually want to put a big Viking baby inside her. Or rather I do, but she might not want that.

I point a finger at her. "Do not move, princess." I climb off the bed to grab a condom from my wallet.

She makes a break for it, rolling off the bed on the opposite side.

I flash a wicked smile as I step to the foot of the bed to block her exit. "You're cornered, princess."

She throws herself on the bed and log rolls across it. I have to hand it to her, she's clever, brave, and agile.

It's hard to imagine how Thompson could've kept her prisoner all these years. I find it odd that a woman as bright, stubborn, and bold as she is wouldn't have found a way out of his clutches before now.

But she won't escape me. I'm a bear. People think we're slow and lumbering, but we pack so much power behind every movement that we can travel great distances in a flash. In one step, I arrive at the side of the bed and catch her as she rolls off.

She gasps in my arms, staring up at me with those big brown eyes.

I have to fight the twitching of my lips as I pretend to frown at her. "Now you earned another spanking, princess."

I toss her back on the bed and roll her to her belly, the pillow perfectly placed under her hips to lift her ass for me.

I give it a few slaps, and she shrieks. I stop and rub away the sting. "Was that what you were looking for, highness?" I squeeze her ass, kneading the soft pillows of her cheeks before delivering three more slaps. "Did you need to feel my hand across your arse?"

"No," she warbles.

"Liar." I roll her over and slide my thumb along her slit, making sure she's still slick and ready for me. My dick aches. I want to bury myself in her perfect pussy.

But this is her first time, and I have to go slow.

"Now I'm going to claim you," I say. We both know I'm playacting. But, damn, if those words don't sound just right.

She shudders at my touch.

I rip open the condom wrapper and roll it on. "I'm going to make it good for you, princess. Just let yourself go and let me take control."

* * *

Paloma

Darius looms over me, his powerful muscles flexing as he braces one hand on the bed.

He's touching me, and I never would've thought his blunt fingers could be so gentle. He parts my folds like he's thumbing open the petals of a flower. He's made me come twice, so I know what he's doing.

I lift my bound wrists, and he catches the tie, pinning it to the bed. His quick movement and casual domination combined with the feeling of being restrained makes heat burst between my legs.

"Oh, you like that," he murmurs. He's teasing my entrance with a slow, circling finger.

"How do you know?"

"You just got wetter." He dips a finger inside me, and adds a second, watching my face. There's an uncomfortable twinge followed by another surge of heat as my body adjusts to the intrusion.

Then he hooks a finger around and rubs my inner wall. My face flushes, and my lips part. My hips rise off the bed as he strokes me in a come-hither motion.

"That's it, princess." He releases my wrist to add another finger. I feel myself squeezing around him. Something's building deep inside me. I have the feeling I'm headed to the tipping point, but I need more stimulation to get there.

"More," I tell him. "I need more."

"Like this?" He adds another finger, and I want to rock forward, pushing them deeper in me.

"It's not enough."

He pulls out his fingers, and I hum my disapproval. He

shows me the glistening digits, then wraps them around his sheathed cock. "Then you're ready for me."

He moves closer, covering me with his body. The wall of muscle fills my vision. I stare at his elegant collarbone, and down to the thick root of his cock. It's huge, long, and thick, nestled in crisp golden hairs. He fists it and rubs the head against me. It's hot and wet, and I know it will be so satisfying.

"Come on," I jerk upwards, and he catches my wrists again.

"Slowly, little dove." My pulse hammers in his hold.

The wide head of his cock pushes against my tight hole, and I suck in a breath at the stretch. I'm not fighting to get more of him inside me, not yet.

Then he does something I don't expect. He dips his head and catches the nape of my neck between his teeth. He kisses the skin there, his rough beard tickling me. I shiver, and he licks over my pulse. That, combined with his thick member penetrating me, is enough to make the volcano inside me start to blow.

"Oh God," I pant. My chest heaves, my nipples get tight and itchy. I arch upwards and rub my breasts against his chest. His coarse hair scratches my tender nipples, and the stimulation adds to the building tension inside me. My whole body starts vibrating, shuddering out of control.

He slides forward, my silky fluids easing his way. It hurts so good. My legs tremble, and I lock them around his powerful hips, urging him forward.

He braces himself over me, every muscle standing out in stark relief. His jaw is rigid, like he's gritting his teeth and forcing himself to conquer me slowly. A red flush creeps over the crests of his cheeks. Under his surly blond brows, his eyes flash amber. He's the most breathtakingly beautiful man I've ever seen.

I glance down. His cock is only halfway inside me. I dig my heels into the dents above his firm buttocks. He slides his hands under my ass, palming the punished skin. He's careful, but the rough calluses on his fingers catch a sore spot. The pain pushes me over the edge.

My orgasm explodes out of me. I come, shaking, and my inner muscles ripple along his shaft. My body clamps down tight, like it wants his cock to become a part of me.

He growls, and the sound rumbles through me, triggering aftershocks. I gasp, trying to catch my breath, when he slides all the way in. I surge to new heights, my climax going on and on.

He dips his head and kisses me. His firm lips move over mine, conquering, dominating. I moan, and he sweeps his tongue into my mouth, thrusting in time with his cock. The rhythm makes delicious tension coil in my belly once more.

"You feel so good, princess," he murmurs against my mouth. I sigh, and he nips at my lips. "You were made to take my cock."

Oh, my God. Am I coming again? I don't think I've stopped.

He's buried deep, pumping into me slowly. I move with him, letting my body stretch, so he can settle flush against my thighs. I never knew I could let someone in like this. I never knew it would feel so amazing.

The hair on his chest chafes my soft skin. I buck against him, needing more stimulation.

"Easy, little dove. I'll give you anything you need."

He pushes up to an elbow and sets his large hand against my neck. He squeezes lightly, in time to the surge of his hips. It should feel like a threat. Instead, it feels good, like instead of collaring me, he's set me free.

My pussy clenches, squeezing his dick, and he groans. His head falls back, his hair falling around his face. It's somehow shoulder length now. He looks like a Viking warrior.

"I'm close," he grits out. I dig my nails into his back, wanting to mark him. His eyes flash with a bright, inhuman light. "Come with me." He grips my throat harder, punctuating the order. At the same time, he slams into me, sending me soaring. The slap of his body against mine stimulates my clit. Stars burst behind my eyes.

He growls as he comes. His dick pulses deep within me, filling the condom with his cum.

"Paloma," he groans, and I shut my eyes, overwhelmed by the reverence in his voice.

He pulls out of me, rising above me in all his tanned and sexy glory. My legs fall open, showing him my freshly fucked pussy. His huge sheathed cock is still hard, shining with my juices, and damn if I don't want him to grip my hair and guide it into my mouth. Forcing me to taste our combined essence.

"Now you belong to me," he rumbles. "Say it."

"I belong to you." I know it's part of the fantasy, that it's not real, but I feel a connection sizzle between us as I say the words.

The Viking plundered me. And I want more.

Chapter Seven

*P*aloma

Darius tugs the tie binding my wrists, releasing them. He rubs the red bands his bowtie left on my skin and kisses my fingers. He leaves for a moment and returns without the condom, carrying a glass of cold water that he offers to me.

I drink thirstily as he strokes his large palm over my body. He left marks all over me. My chest is chafed pink, and there's some faint redness lingering on my ass from my punishment. He fusses over them, and the sight of my Viking giant frowning at a faint bruise on my hip is enough to make me swoon.

He puts a hand on my belly, cupping my curves. I should feel self-conscious about my belly, but I don't. Darius makes me feel like my body is perfect, exactly as it is. "You okay?"

"Better than okay. That was...amazing." There aren't words in any language to describe how good it felt. "Thank you."

"It was my honor." He looks so serious.

I lean forward and kiss his chin. He cups my head in his large hands, looking deeply into my eyes. I stare back, studying the gold-flecked gray of his pupils. They were shining so brightly during sex, but it must have been a trick of the light. And was his beard always this bushy?

My stomach growls loudly, breaking the moment.

Darius chuckles and kisses my forehead. His scratchy beard tickles me.

"I'm going to see if I can get some food for my princess."

I start to push up to say I'll come with him, but he rolls me to my side and swats my ass. "Stay."

I sink back into the plush bed, savoring the languor in my limbs.

But the moment he disappears behind the door, reality sets in.

I had my fun. I chose and controlled who took my virginity and how. It was incredible. Better than I ever could've imagined.

But our moment is over.

Thom will have every brute on his payroll out looking for me. Not to mention, he still has my sister. My body goes cold thinking of what he might do to Wren if he doesn't hear from me soon. Right now, she's on a choir tour with school, but he might try to snatch her while she's on the road and make good on his threat.

I want my freedom, but I'm not willing to trade her life for mine.

And I don't want Darius' death on my conscience, either.

I have to act. I rise and put on Darius' black button down over my skimpy pajamas. I search his pants for the car keys but come up with nothing.

No matter. We're in an area of vacation homes, but

there's bound to be some traffic on the main road. I just need to get to a phone, so I can call Thom and stop the bomb from ticking.

I don't have much time.

I hear Darius out on the porch that faces the ocean. He's talking on his phone. "Thanks, man," he says. "I appreciate it." He turns away, facing the sea.

I use the opportunity to dash through the house. There's a side door in the kitchen, and I make for that, pausing when the light glints off some metal. I found the car keys.

I take the time to leave a quick note.

Thank you for rescuing me, dear Viking, but I have to go back. I will make a bargain with Thom to keep you safe or convince him it was a drunken escapade.

Besos,
Paloma

Slipping out the door to the garage, I hesitate. I don't actually know how to drive because Thom didn't allow me to learn. Too bad there's not a stable around here–I'm way more comfortable on a horse.

But how hard can driving a car be?

I hit the button to open the garage door. Ack! I didn't know it would be so loud. Darius will definitely hear. I run for the stolen sports car, climb behind the wheel and adjust the seat way closer, so my feet reach the pedals.

But how does the keyless fob work? I press buttons until the car roars to life, then I adjust the gear to the R button. Or I try to. It won't move. I shake the handle.

My foot presses one of the pedals, and suddenly the lever moves.

My heart pounds as I pull it down to the R and step harder on the pedal.

Nothing.

Okay. Other pedal. I floor it.

That one works. The car lurches, tires screaming on the garage floor as the car flies out of the garage way too fast.

I hit something.

Oh shit.

Oh shit! I clap my hand over my mouth. It's Darius.

I throw open the car door, but the car lurches again.

Darius's hands are braced against the back spoiler, and he has the rear wheels lifted off the ground to keep it from moving.

"Put it in park! The P," he barks.

I shove the handle to P, and the car lurches again, then stops.

Darius lowers the rear tires as I climb back out. He arches a sexy brow. "Going somewhere, princess?"

I suck in a breath, considering whether to tell him the truth or lie.

No, he deserves the truth. I just don't want him to play hero for me and end up dead.

"I have to go back."

* * *

Darius

"What?"

My bear tries to rip free of the hold I have on him. He's going insane over Paloma trying to leave.

Over the fact that she wants to *go back.*

90

He wants to rampage, ripping his claws through the walls of the garage Paloma drove halfway out of.

"No," I say before she can explain. "No fucking way you're going back."

"Darius, there's more to this than you understand. Thom has leverage on me."

Everything in me goes still. A dark prick of warning seeps under the rage of my bear.

"What do you mean?"

"He has my sister. He said if I tried to escape again, she'd die."

Ice sluices through my veins. I grind my teeth together. "Where is she?"

"At a boarding school in Connecticut."

I nod. "Then we'll get to her first."

"*No.* You don't understand." She's not soothed by my words.

"Explain it to me."

"They don't allow cell phones at her school, and it only has school intranet, so I can't get a message to her."

"Then we'll go there. Connecticut is just an hour away."

"It's more complicated than that. She's on a school choir trip to Ireland right now. We need to figure out how to find her before Thom does."

Fuck.

Paloma is all warrior. Her jaw is set with determination. Her eyes flash with anger. She may have been a princess in a tower, but she's no wilting flower.

"Also, I'll die without my medicine. We have two days until I go into full cardiac arrest."

My bear tries to claw out of me in a rage.

Stay. Down.

Fuck. The medicine that smells like toxic. I should've remembered that.

"Okay. We'll get your medication. What's it called? My brother's a doctor–he can call a prescription in somewhere for you."

She shakes her head. "It's not a standard prescription. Dr. Handel compounds it himself. Some kind of proprietary blend."

My brows slam down. "What is your exact diagnosis?"

"It's a form of hemophilia."

"Okay. We'll get you medicine for it. And we'll find your sister." I look around, not liking us being out in the open, especially with a stolen car's plates visible to anyone who drives by. "Let's go inside and find something to eat. We will both make better decisions when we're properly nourished."

Paloma looks around but finally nods, and my bear eases back on the choke-hold he has on me.

"I'm right behind you–I'm just going to pull the car back in." I call Kylie Jackson, a cat shifter hacker who lives in Tucson. She's known in the shifter world as a fixer of sorts.

Paloma has already pulled a box of macaroni and cheese and a can of tuna from the pantry and is heating a pot of water.

"Listen, I need a favor," I say to her after reminding her who I am. "It's a matter of life and death. I need help locating a student at a boarding school in Connecticut–one that limits communication with the outside world, so she doesn't have a cell phone."

"That shouldn't be too big of a problem."

"Well, to add to the dilemma, they're on a field trip to Ireland."

"No problem. That means there will be a document trail through customs."

"You can hack into customs?"

"Of course. What's the student's name?"

Paloma stands close to me, listening. "Wren Castillo."

"Wren Castillo," Kylie repeats, her shifter hearing picking up Paloma's voice through the phone. "I'll see what I can find. And one of my contacts is on the way to drop off groceries and some clothes."

"Thanks again. I owe you, big time."

"Yes, you do," Kylie agrees, but I'm not worried about owing her or her wolf mate a favor.

Wolves aren't crazy in the head like vampires. Owing a wolf isn't anything to fear. I'm friendly with her mate Jackson King and the other billionaire wolf shifter, Brick Blackthroat. His cousin Aiden Adalwulf is another story. He's more of the Thom Thompson kind of creepy.

The water starts to boil, and Paloma empties the box of macaroni into the pot and sets the oven timer for eight minutes.

I step up behind her and rest my hands lightly on her hips. "So, what am I missing, Rapunzel? Thompson is a sex trafficker?" I ask. "Are there other women he's auctioned off?"

She shakes her head. "No."

"Just you? Why now? What's so special about your virginity?"

Paloma turns toward the stove, hiding her face.

I knew there was something else she hadn't told me. It's something she doesn't want to tell me.

I step right up behind her. "What is Thompson up to?" I keep my voice low.

She rotates slowly to face me. Her hands come up to my

chest. I'm not sure whether she's going to push me away or tip her face up for a kiss. She hesitates.

"You can trust me, Paloma–whatever it is. I can help you better if I understand what's going on."

She draws in a breath and nods, like she made up her mind. "Do you know that movie where the kid sees dead people?"

"*Sixth Sense?* Yeah."

"I see dead companies."

My eyebrows rise. "What do you mean?"

"When I was in eighth grade, our economics teacher gave us paper accounts to make stock trades. We discovered I have a knack for it. I have this intuition about companies that are going to go out of business, and I learned to make short sales on them."

"In *eighth grade?*"

Paloma laughs. "Yes. My mom was a trader, so I'd grown up with stock trading in my blood. She was so proud of my success that she showed my paper account to her boss."

"Thompson."

"Yes. He offered to mentor me. He wanted to find out my methodology. Of course, I didn't have one–it was all intuitive."

Paloma's eyes cloud, and she folds her arms across her chest, protectively.

I squeeze her shoulders. No wonder Thom has the most successful hedge fund in the world. He found a talented psychic and enslaved her.

"Our parents died in a car accident not long after that. Thom told me this weekend that he had them killed." She shivers, and I draw her into my arms, pulling her cheek against my chest.

"Fuck, Paloma. That's horrible."

"And then he locked me up. I've been trading for him ever since. He holds Wren's liberty and now *her very life* over my head to keep me from running away. I barely get to talk to her. My only pleasure is our Sunday video calls." She shrugs. "And riding Starlight on the weekends." She lifts her big brown eyes to my face. "And historical romance. You know–fantasizing about a giant Viking taking my virginity."

I smile at her flirtation, but my smile quickly fades when I realize just how horrific her life has been. I don't know how she can even keep things light.

"So the auction wasn't just about your virginity."

"No, it was supposed to be a lease of my stock trading services via a fake engagement to the winner. The engagement will be broken off in a year, when the winner returns me to Thom.

"I tried to escape Thursday night, but Thom caught me. That's when he told me he would kill Wren if I ran away again. And last night is when he revealed that the auction was for my virginity as well. The intention is to *breed me* to produce equally talented stock traders."

"That is... sick. Utterly twisted."

"I thought you were one of the men who wanted to bid on me."

"I knew nothing about it. I hope you believe that."

"No, I do. I have good instincts. I secretly hoped you'd be the winner because something about you made me feel safe."

My heart gallops. How did this human suddenly become my whole world?

"You *are* safe. There's no fucking way I'm letting you go back to Lockepoint. We will find your sister, and we will get your medication. Then we'll figure out how to take Thom

95

Thompson down once and for all." My bear rumbles in agreement. I shush him and rub my belly, hoping to pass off the noise as my empty stomach.

The timer goes off, and Paloma picks up the pot from the stove and pours the water off the macaroni shells. She stirs in the cheese and some of the cream from the box she opened this morning for our coffee.

I find a can opener and open the can of tuna she pulled out. We stir it into the macaroni and cheese to make a poor man's one pot dinner.

"I feel like I'm in college again," I say as I try a bite, eating straight from the pot. Then I remember that Paloma didn't get to go to college, and my bear nearly erupts to the surface. I grit my teeth and bend my head, fighting to push him back.

"Yeah? Where did you go?" Paloma serves herself a bowl of food and takes it to the breakfast table, nestled in a window nook that overlooks the ocean. She's busy eating. She doesn't seem to notice my struggle.

I follow her with the pot. "First, a small community college near where I grew up. Then to business school at Columbia." My bear recedes enough for me to pick up the pot and shovel in some food.

"Where did you grow up?"

"New Mexico." I don't like talking about my childhood, but sharing with Paloma feels right. "In the mountains."

"I've never seen the mountains," she says. "I've always wanted to." I could kill Thom for what he's robbed from her. My teeth ache, growing thicker. My bear is ready to bite someone's head off. Literally. "Maybe one day you could take me."

My heart does a double-pump. She's planning a future

for us. Except...I'm not safe for her. Not long-term. My bear is already too volatile being around her.

"Maybe." I hate to sound so ambivalent, but I vowed not to return to my home. It's too dangerous. Out in the wild, my bear is stronger. He might take control and not give it back.

Her face shutters. She finishes her food and takes her bowl to the sink to rinse it. "Well, let's focus on getting Wren away from Thom. After that, who knows? We'll have to go into hiding."

I can't ignore the grim determination in her voice and, beneath it, the thread of despair. I go to her and stand at her back, reaching around her to put the pot in the sink. I help her finish the washing then brace my hands against the counter, caging her in. "It's going to be okay," I murmur into her ear.

"How do you know?"

"I'm going to keep you safe." I stroke back her hair, baring her neck. The scent of orchids rises from her skin, and my mouth waters.

Claim her.

The instinct rocks through me with more conviction this time. I tighten my grip on the counter to keep from pulling her close. It's not just my bear wrestling for control. It feels more like all of me.

Like Paloma really is my fated mate.

Damn.

It must be true.

That explains why I just risked losing my entire company and everything I fought so hard to win on Wall Street to save her. But it doesn't change anything.

I can't claim a human. My bear is too wild. I've never even allowed myself a relationship, in case I lose control.

The most I can have is this moment of closeness, sharing my body heat and comfort with this incredible woman. Paloma leans back into me. Her head doesn't come up to my chin. I close my arms around her, savoring the feel of her in my arms.

"I wish..."

"What do you wish?"

Instead of answering, she grips the counter and lets out a little moan. She sags against me.

I turn her to face me. Her eyes are glassy. "Paloma?"

"I don't feel so good–" Her eyes roll up, and she slumps.

"Paloma!" I carry her to the couch and lay her out. She's unconscious, her arm limp when I lift it and let it fall. I feel for her pulse, and it flutters against my fingers.

She told me she was sick and needed medicine to forestall her collapse. I thought we'd have more time.

I need to get her to a doctor, one I trust.

And there's only one person on earth that fits that description.

I pull out my phone and dial Sully. "I need another favor. It's an emergency." I explain my plan while getting Paloma into the car, and Sully promises to make arrangements.

"Hang on, princess." I strap her in and kiss her forehead. Her skin has turned clammy to the touch.

I'll break all speed records getting us to the tiny airstrip where Sully will have a private jet waiting. From there, it'll be a direct flight to New Mexico.

There's just one call left to make.

"Darius? Is that you, brother?"

"Matthias." I brace myself for his anger, but he only sounds curious. "I need your help. I'm bringing someone to you. A human. She needs medical attention. She's...important to me."

There's a pause. It's probably only seconds long, but it feels like years. I watch Paloma's chest rise and fall with labored breaths.

Finally Matthias says, "Does that mean..."

I'm breaking my self-imposed exile and going back to where I vowed I'd never return.

Back to Bad Bear Mountain.

"Yes, brother. I'm coming home."

Chapter Eight

Paloma

P A tapping sound wakes me. I crack my eyes open and squint against the brightness. The blurred shapes sharpen and become a set of green curtains framing a window filled with cheerful sunlight.

There's a faint pain in my head, and my chest aches, but other than that, I feel okay. I move my limbs and everything seems to be working.

I sit up. I'm in a big bed that fills a tiny room. The walls are brown logs, and the floor is made of rough hewn pine wood planks stained a honey brown. I push back the heavy plaid blanket covering me and notice the green sheet set matches the curtains, the fabric patterned with tiny brown bears.

The only other furniture is a small bedside table and lamp, and there's also an IV with a bag full of clear liquid. A small bandage in the crook of my right elbow tells me that someone put a needle in me at one point.

There's no sign of Darius or anyone else. I'm in a log

cabin that smells of pine and smoke, and someone's been playing doctor.

I don't know what's going on, but I'm going to escape. Voices murmur behind the big closed door, so I swing my feet off the bed in the direction of the window.

I have to pause and close my eyes against a wave of dizziness. Have I been drugged? Or am I just weak from the medicine?

As soon as I can, I push up from the bed. I'm in nothing but a faded flannel shirt. It's half buttoned and so large that when I stand up straight, it falls to mid thigh.

Tap, tap, tap, something goes at the window. I pad barefoot to see the shining dark head of a raven pop up and peck at the thick glass with its black beak. It turns its head and lets out a squawk, then flies off in a flurry of wings.

Weird.

The cabin window offers a view of a tufted meadow lined with rows of pine trees. Beyond the snowy boughs is a rolling mountain vista, magnificent under a clear, blue sky.

It's breathtaking. And horrifying. How did I get here? How long have I been passed out?

A small draft comes in from the cracks around the window. I shiver and take a step back but not before a huge shadow falls across me. I can't be sure of what I'm seeing until a huge furry head ducks down, and the creature stares at me with beady black eyes.

I shriek and back away from the window. I've never seen a bear outside of a zoo, and here it is, staring like it's thinking about smashing a paw through the window, so it can eat me.

The door behind me bursts open. "Paloma?" It's Darius.

I stagger to him, and he scoops me up. "What is it? What's wrong?"

"Oh!" I try to catch my breath, feeling foolish for screaming bloody murder. "There was a bear." I point. "Looking in the window." The bear's gone from the window, but I see it lumbering across the snowy field. It's massive. I had no idea bears could get that big.

"It's okay," Darius soothes me. "He's probably more afraid of you than you are of him."

He?

"You can put me down. I was just startled, that's all."

Darius seems reluctant to set me back down on the rough-hewn wooden floor of the little cabin, but he does. I watch as the bear reaches the end of the field and rises to hind paws. A small, dark shape swoops down. The raven lands on its shoulder.

What? Why does this feel like I'm in a fairy tale? I went from Rapunzel to Snow White.

The two creatures disappear into the trees.

"Wh-where are we?" I turn back to Darius. He's clean shaven now, and out of the tuxedo ensemble that made me swoon. Now he's drool-worthy in the complete opposite vibe: a thick flannel shirt and a faded pair of jeans. His feet are bare. The light blue and tan plaid matches the shirt I'm wearing.

"New Mexico. Bad Bear Mountain."

My mind spins, trying to assimilate it all. The last thing I remember is standing with him in the kitchen at a beach-front safe house in Rhode Island. Now we're two thousand miles away on...did he say... *Bad Bear* Mountain?

"*Why?*" I splutter at the same moment I remember that *bad bear* was also the safe word he gave me.

This must be his home.

"You passed out, and I had to get you medical care."

"In *New Mexico?*"

"Medical care with someone I trust."

"Right. Your brother." It's all coming back to me. He'd said his brother could prescribe something for me.

"Yes."

"Did he...did he find the right prescription?"

Darius' expression is troubled. "I'm going to let him tell you what he found."

I blink. "No, you tell me. What is it?"

"Come here." Darius takes my hand and leads me out of the tiny bedroom and into the living room of the cabin.

A wood fire burns in the grate, making the room cozy. At the kitchen table sits a man, wearing a crisp white button-down shirt and black-framed glasses. He stands when we emerge, and I realize he's even taller than Darius. Other than their height, though, I see no resemblance. They are obviously not full brothers if they're biologically related. His skin is dark brown, and he's more slender than Darius.

"Paloma." The man has a voice as deep as my Viking's. "I'm glad to see you're awake."

"This is my brother, Matthias." Darius ushers me forward with a reassuring hand at my lower back.

I extend my palm and shake Matthias' hand. "Thank you for caring for me."

"Of course. Are you feeling more like yourself?"

"I feel a bit weak and dizzy," I admit. "Were you able to match my medication?"

"Yes, about that." He wears the same troubled expression Darius had.

"What is it?" I look from one tall man to the other. The way the hairs prickle on my arm tells me something is very wrong.

Maybe my condition is fatal–worse than Thom made it

104

seem. Maybe that's why he wanted to breed me—to ensure he had someone to carry on my work when I'm gone.

My stomach twists and a wave of nausea rolls through me. When I sway on my feet, Darius loops an arm around my waist, his large palm settling on my hip to steady me.

"Paloma, I don't believe you're sick at all." Matthias adjusts his glasses. "I found a large quantity of anticoagulant in your system, along with several chemical compounds that could cause dizziness and extreme fatigue."

"Anticoagulant? That wouldn't make sense for hemophilia."

"No, it wouldn't." Darius sounds grim.

I stare at him, not understanding.

"Paloma, I don't think the medication your doctor administered was to treat any disease," Matthias says. "I believe it was poison intended to make you dependent."

"But the hemophilia?"

Matthias shakes his head. "You don't have hemophilia. I gave you a dose of a medicine I compound here that promotes rapid healing. It will help the effects of the poison wear off quickly, and then time will tell. I suspect you will return to perfect health."

I consider myself strong. I've had to be for Wren. I don't ever waste time crying or feeling sorry for myself. But my vision goes wavy with tears of rage at this fresh betrayal.

"I...I'm not sick? I never was sick?" The little cabin is suddenly too hot and stuffy for me.

I lose a hot tear down my cheek before I can blink it back.

Darius bands his thick forearm around my waist, holding me up from behind.

I push him off, though. I'm too mad for anyone to touch me right now. "I need–" I look around desperately.

Darius studies me with concern. "What do you need, princess? Whatever it is, it's yours."

I'm so tired of feeling trapped. "I need to get out–to go for a walk."

"Of course. Let's find you some pants." Darius reaches for my hand, then wisely lets it drop to his side as he heads back to the bedroom. I follow.

"I would suggest rest, food, and fluids, but fresh air makes sense, too," Matthias says mildly to our backs.

In the bedroom, Darius pulls open drawers, making grumbling noises as he roots through the clothes.

"Is this Matthias' house?"

Darius pulls out a long pair of sweatpants. "No. It's the spare cabin."

"It's your cabin, brother," Matthias calls from the living room. Apparently, sound carries despite the thick log walls.

Darius gives an irritated shake of his head. "This isn't my home," he calls back. He holds out the sweatpants. "These will be way too long, but there's a drawstring to keep the waist up. We can walk over to Teddy's, so you can borrow something of Lana's."

I yank on the sweatpants, still itchy as hell to get outside. "Who's Lana?" I demand, as if Darius is the bad guy, keeping secrets from me.

I know he's not. I know I can trust him, but after finding out Thom has been poisoning me for years, I feel the need to arm myself with agency, information, and independence. The time for playing captured maiden is over. I'm the marauding warrior now, and I'm going after Thom Thompson for everything he's done to me.

"My sister-in-law."

"So Teddy's your brother."

"Yeah."

"You have two brothers?"

"Seven."

I look up from knotting the drawstring in surprise. "Wow. Your poor parents. I'll bet it was rowdy around here when you were young."

"Just a mom. She adopted all eight of us. And yeah– rowdy is an understatement."

I'm already calming down just hearing about Darius' family. Just from his steadying presence in the room.

He hands me two thick pairs of woolen socks. "I'm not sure my hiking boots are going to stay on your feet, but we can try."

I sit on the bed and pull on both pairs of socks, then stuff my feet in the giant boots he set at my feet. My foot comes out the moment I take a step. "Screw it," I say, and march out in the doubled up wool socks. They will keep my feet warm and protected. If I don't get outside, I'm going to burst.

Darius trails me out the front cabin door and drapes a huge puffy coat around my shoulders. I tug it on as I march off the wooden porch. I stop once I'm in the woods, stop to gaze up at the towering pine trees. The air smells crisp and clean. Heavenly.

A chill bites my cheeks, but even that feels good. I'm not trapped. Darius isn't holding me prisoner. I'm in the woods under a cool blue sky.

"I need to get to Wren."

"I'm working on it, princess. I've called in favors from everyone I know, and so have my brothers. The best hackers in the world are digging into Thom and all his companies. They'll find where she is in Ireland, and we'll get to her before he does."

107

My body relaxes. I trust Darius to do all he can to find her. "Thank you."

"Of course." He peers at me. "How are you feeling?"

"Better, now that I'm not being poisoned. *Que cabrón*. I can't believe that *pendejo*."

"We'll make him pay." Darius sounds grim and determined. I'm with him, but I need a moment to savor my freedom.

I turn and take Darius' hand. "Show me around?"

My Viking flashes a devastating smile. "My pleasure." He leads me on a trail that curves down and meets another footpath. His boots crunch fallen leaves. Birds flutter to and fro as if unafraid of us. It's so different from Lockepoint. From the East coast.

"Are there a lot of bears in these woods?" I ask. I'm glad we're staying on a well-worn trail.

"Uh..." Darius seems caught off-guard. "A fair amount."

"Really?" my reply comes out a squeak. "Are they all as big as the one I saw?"

"That one is the biggest," he assures me. Which isn't reassuring at all. "Let's keep walking," he says like he's trying to change the subject.

I narrow my eyes at him but let him lead me further.

A chorus of shouts burst out. There's something happening in the field beyond a belt of pine trees. I quicken my steps to find out what's going on, but Darius seems reluctant to follow.

"Incoming!" someone shouts.

I step out onto the field just as a blurred shape darts past me. A tall, shirtless guy in a kilt runs full tilt into the forest, turning at the last minute to catch a big white ball. He crash lands onto a bush, but holds up the ball. "Got it!"

"Watch where you're going," Darius snarls. He inserts

himself between me and the ball player, quicker than I can blink.

"Sorry, Darius," the guy calls, throwing a curious look my way as he trots back on the field to join the other players.

There are four of them, all tall and broad-shouldered, and incredibly muscular. The shirtless one, the guy who crashed into the bush, has a chest that's a jaw-dropping maze of muscles.

The players line up facing each other, two on two. Three of the four wear kilts. One has a poofy white pirate shirt and a red kilt, another has a poofy black pirate shirt that matches his black kilt. A third has a red kilt and no shirt. The fourth is dressed more normally, in a black t-shirt that shows off the tattoos covering his arms from the wrist up.

At some unseen signal, the shirtless one tosses the ball behind him to his teammate in jeans. The kilt-wearing opponents charge forward, but get blocked by the shirtless guy, who tackles them hard enough to slam them into the ground.

I wince, but they all spring to their feet.

"Canyon, what the hell?" shouts the one in the black kilt. "We've told you a thousand times. No tackling in rugby."

"There *is* tackling. But we're supposed to tackle him." The one in the white shirt points to the tattooed player, who has strolled up to a nearby tree. He punts the ball through two forked branches, then pulls out a blunt from his pocket and lights it.

"Awww, Axel. No smoking 'til the end of the game, you promised," the three kilted players chorus. The three of them all have sandy brown hair and pale, freckled skin and appear the same age. They're all the same height and build, too. They don't look identical, but there's a close resemblance.

The player near us blows out a cloud of skunky-smoke. He's leaner than the other three and handsome as a movie star. His long black hair is pulled back into a ponytail. His t-shirt proudly proclaims that Triumph motorcycles are the best in the world.

"Hey, Darius," he greets us. "Hey, Darius' lady."

"Axel," Darius puts his arm around my waist. "This is Paloma."

"Nice to meet you," I say.

Axel offers me the blunt, and I decline with a wave of a hand.

The three kilted players crowd around. They're all so tall, I feel like I've shrunk. "Hey, aren't you going to introduce us?"

"Paloma, these are the triplets. Hutch," Darius points to the one in the white shirt, "and Bern." He points to the one in the black shirt.

"What about me?" The shirtless one pushes between the other two. Up close, his chest is even more amazing. Sweat runs down the grooves of his muscles and darkens the light hair at his temples.

"Put on a shirt, and I'll think about it," Darius growls.

"Canyon." The shirtless one puts a hand to his chest. "Mi'lady." The triplets all bow.

I stifle a laugh. They're all so huge and adorable.

Darius squeezes me closer. He's being all possessive, but I don't hate it. "These are my stupid brothers."

"Oh," I make a mental note. The triplets and Axel all seem younger than Darius and Matthias.

"How many of us has she met?" Bern asks.

"Five. She met Matthias back at the cabin."

110

"Has she met Teddy?" Canyon asks.

Darius stiffens at the mention of his twin. "Not yet."

Hutch says, "That just leaves–"

Branches snap behind us, and I turn to see the bear from this morning pushing through the bushes. Darius doesn't seem worried, but I clutch at him. The bear rises to hind legs and offers Axel the rugby ball. Axel calmly accepts it. He's got the blunt sticking out of the corner of his mouth. I get that not much fazes him, but no one else is freaking out at the fact a giant bear is standing right next to us. And it apparently knows how to play catch.

Just me.

"Holy shit," I breathe.

"It's okay," says Hutch. "It's just–"

Bern elbows him in the gut, and he doubles over.

"Just a random bear–" Bern assures me.

"Our pet bear," Canyon says at the same time.

"Uh yeah, our *pet*," Hutch adds, rubbing the spot where Bern elbowed him. "He escaped from the zoo."

The bear cocks its head at them. It looks faintly disapproving. Then it drops to all fours and lumbers away. It moves silently, and remarkably fast for such a giant animal.

I shudder, and Darius covers my shoulder with his huge hand. The weight is comforting. He dips his head and murmurs, "Welcome to Bad Bear Mountain."

* * *

Darius

"Your brothers are sweet," Paloma tells me. We're back at the cabin, and I'm making us salmon on the grill. I was going to walk up to Teddy's, but her stomach started to growl, and I was happy to cut our walk short and put off meeting my twin.

Now we're blissfully alone. Matthias has gone to his shift at the hospital, and I managed to communicate to the triplets that Paloma and I needed some space. Axel wandered off, probably to work on one of his perpetual projects–either a car or a motorcycle. And I told Hutch and Bern to keep Everest busy. Two bear sightings in one day is enough. If he wants to meet Paloma, he needs to show up in human form.

"They can be," I grunt. "But mostly they're assholes. Especially my twin."

Paloma's head pops up. "You have a twin?"

"Yeah, Teddy."

"Does he look like you?"

I nod. "Identical."

"When do I get to meet him?" Paloma's sitting at the picnic table, her head propped on her hands. She's got a healthy color to her cheeks and looks more alive and relaxed than I've seen her.

"Hopefully never."

She chuckles like I'm joking, but I'm not. Teddy's home on the mountain, but Matthias said Lana's pregnancy is making him grouchier than usual.

I hope he lies low. Whenever we meet, we fight. Combining his bad mood with the way I'm amped up to protect Paloma would lead to World War III.

I keep checking my phone.

Paloma looks up when it buzzes as a text comes through. "Any word about Wren's location?"

"Not yet, but my associate, Kylie, is working on it. Her mate–husband–owns the top infosecurity company, and she's one of the best hackers in the world. If anyone can find

Wren, it's her."

"What did she say?"

"She's working on hacking the school's computers to link up to Wren's school-issued laptop."

The tension returns to Paloma's face, and I would do anything to wipe it away.

"The clock is ticking. What if he's already pulled her from the trip? Or–"

"Don't go there," I say firmly. "We *will* find her."

"I should call him. Promise to turn myself in–just to buy us more time."

"No," I growl. "No way. That would give him the chance to make demands we aren't willing to meet."

"*We?*" Paloma searches my face.

My chest tightens. I can't be part of a *we*. Not when my bear is so destructive. I would end up harming Paloma, like I hurt our biological mom–and she was a bear. She healed. If I hurt Paloma I would never forgive myself. I'd rather die.

But there's no way I'm going to let her feel like she's alone in this, either.

"Yes, *we*. I'm in this with you, princess. We will see this through together."

And then I will have to let you go.

My bear nearly breaks free at that. I have to turn away to hide my glowing eyes from her. Breathe deeply and clench my fists to keep him down. He's been clawing to get out ever since we got here.

Bringing Paloma here, to the mountain, makes my bear think he's going to claim her. Mark her as my fated mate. The only reason I've held him off, I suspect, is because he recognizes Paloma needs to heal. Still, the need to mark her is growing by the minute.

As if what's going on with Thompson and finding Wren wasn't complicated enough.

I serve up the salmon and pause to watch her take the first few bites. I fucking love feeding her. It soothes my bear.

She wriggles in her seat. "It's delicious. Thank you."

"Better than tuna mac and cheese, at least."

Her soft laugh does strange things to my chest.

I check the potatoes I have roasting in aluminum foil. They're almost done. The wind picks up, chapping Paloma's cheeks.

"We can go inside, if you're cold," I offer, settling onto the picnic bench opposite her

She wipes her lips on a napkin. "I enjoy being outside." After years of captivity, going where she wants must feel glorious.

For a moment, I feel guilty. I've been keeping my bear captive, locked down. No wonder he's straining to break free.

Then I remember what he's done, the mayhem that drove both my mothers away. Caging him is the only option.

Paloma and I are almost done with our meal when I catch a scent that makes me stiffen. I shoot out of my seat so quickly, Paloma drops her fork.

"Darius? What–"

"Brother!" an angry shout cuts her off. Twenty feet off, in the forest, a tall pine shudders and falls, crashing to the ground. In a flash, I'm standing between Paloma and the treeline.

A bear-growl rockets from my throat.

My twin strides out, lightning flashing in his eyes. His bear is out of control.

"What the fuck are you doing?" He points from me to Paloma.

"Theodore." I shove my bear back down. I am the civilized one. I keep my bear on lock in a city packed with humans. I won't let him goad me into my animal nature.

I raise both hands, keeping my voice at a reasonable volume. "Calm down."

"My mate is pregnant, and you brought danger to the mountain," he spits. "Now you're going to answer to me."

"I had no choice, Teddy. You know that."

"You don't even have the decency to say you'll come home for Thanksgiving, but the moment you want to show off to some Manhattan *socialite–*"

I charge before I even know what I'm doing. I'm still in human form, but civility just blew up. My bear wants blood for him speaking about Paloma like she's nothing. I tackle Teddy to the ground and take a swing at his face.

"Darius!" Paloma screams when I crack him in the jaw.

Teddy log rolls his way on top and punches me in the ribs. "You won't be happy until you destroy our mountain," he roars.

I block his punch to my face.

"This is our home, and you're not welcome if you can't respect it. I have a cub to protect now." He punches my ribs, right and left.

I could give a shit about the mountain right now. "You think your mate is more important than mine?" I shoot my feet in the air to toss Teddy off as I back roll to my feet. "*Do you?*" I snarl.

"Darius, stop!" Paloma shouts. She's right beside me, which further enrages my bear. He doesn't want Teddy's fists anywhere near her.

"*Is* she your mate?" Teddy comes at me, swinging. I dodge and jab him in the kidney. "You haven't marked her. She doesn't even know what you are."

My bear roars at the idea of marking her. He's already so close to the surface, I lose even more control.

"I can't." I don't know if I'm telling my bear or Teddy. All I know is I have to keep a lid on the bear or Paloma will get hurt.

"What does he mean, *what you are?*"

My bear rips free. I feel the change happening.

"Go," I grit out. "Run."

Paloma gasps, her face blanching as she gets a good look at my face. I know what she's seeing–my wild bear, my glowing eyes.

"Let her see it." Teddy wipes the blood from his mouth with the back of his hand, bouncing on the balls of his feet, boxer-style.

"No!" I roar. I have to get away from her. I can't hurt my beautiful mate.

"See what, Darius?" Paloma shrieks. She's angry, but I'm not sure why. Maybe she's afraid.

I'm afraid too. Afraid for her. Afraid of what she'll think of me when she finds out what I am.

"Go now!" I roar and fall to all fours, my spine bowing as I fight my bear.

"He won't hurt you." Teddy holds up a hand at Paloma, who hasn't moved. He keeps his gaze on me, poised for my attack.

This fucking asshole. He made me shift and scare Paloma. I need to regain control, but first...I'm going to make him pay.

My bear gains the upper hand, and I lose the struggle. The air crackles as I change.

"Finally," Teddy snarls.

I rise to my full eight-foot height and roar at Teddy. One warning before I rip him to shreds.

Chapter Nine

Paloma

My jaw hangs open. Darius *is a bear!* A massive, terrifying grizzly bear with a row of gleaming sharp teeth and five-inch claws.

He launches himself at his brother—*who is also a bear!* The two grapple and roll to the ground with vicious roars.

My heart pounds. My feet remain glued to the forest floor despite Darius' commands to run. I don't know whether I'm frozen with fear or fascination. Or just because I refuse to be told what to do ever again.

Mostly, I want Teddy to leave Darius the fuck alone.

"Stop!" I scream, picking up a rock and aiming. I reconsider and drop it—I don't want to hit Darius. I find a big stick instead. I can handle this—I'm around large animals all the time.

"Stop it! Shoo!" I know which one is Teddy by the color of the shreds of the shirt that hang in rags around his neck. I smack him over the head. "Go away."

As soon as the wood cracks over that massive skull, I realize what a huge mistake I made. This is a grizzly bear, not a horse. Not that I would hit a horse. But this bear could kill me with one swipe of that massive paw.

But, shockingly, Teddy makes a warbling sound and drops to all fours, ducking his head away from me.

"That's right," I yell, emboldened. "Go! Go home!" I poke him with the end of the stick. "Bad bear!"

He grabs the branch and breaks it in a very human-like move, and for a moment, I think I've gone too far, but then he wheels and bounds away in the same direction he came.

I stare after him in shock, and then a hysterical giggle comes out of my mouth. "A bad bear" –I cover my mouth to hold in the fit of giggles– "on Bad Bear Mountain."

When I turn to face down Darius, though, I find a naked man in place of the bear. A glorious, muscled Viking man.

He's panting, his expression strained, his fists and teeth clenched as if in concentration. He stalks toward me, eyes still gleaming gold, and lifts me into his arms, making me feel as light as a feather.

Now I know why I'm not too heavy for Darius. He's not human. His bear probably likes his woman to have some meat on her bones. He'd crack one of those waiflike models Thom wanted me to look like in half.

"Can't–" He seems unable to speak. He carries me up the steps of the cabin.

My brain reels and crashes into a brick wall, recognizing anew that *my lover is a bear*. I've heard of werewolves. I didn't know about bears.

"Not–" Darius tries again. "...not safe," he mutters. "You're not safe with me."

Maybe I should be afraid. Maybe Teddy was trying to get Darius to bite me and turn me into a werewolf like them. I mean bear. Werebear.

Oh my God—what is happening right now?

This can't be real!

Except I'm certain that I *am* safe. Yes, my pulse is racing from adrenaline pumping through my veins, but no part of me believes Darius would hurt me. I didn't even believe it when he was a giant grizzly bear.

Plus, Teddy said he wouldn't hurt me.

But Darius seems to think he will.

"This isn't right. I didn't want you to see that." Darius carries me to the bedroom. "Lock the door. Lock me out. You're not safe with him." He tries to set me down, but I cling to his neck and wrap my legs around his waist.

"Not safe with whom? Teddy?"

"With me." He walks over to the bed and tries to deposit me, but I still refuse to be put down. If he thinks I'm going to be locked in a bedroom again—even if it's for my safety—he's delusional.

"I'm safe here."

"Not with me. Not with my bear."

I lean my forehead against his creased one. "I'm okay," I murmur against his skin. As if he were my horse, Starlight, spooked by something on a ride, I hold the presence of quiet for him. "I'm okay. Nothing bad happened. We're okay here together now."

He climbs onto the bed with me still in his arms and lowers us together, his naked body covering mine. We lock eyes. His still have the wild glow of amber—I understand now what I've been seeing. Darius isn't human—he is something altogether different. Maybe that's why I was so drawn to him from the very beginning.

I sensed he was nothing like the wretched men who have surrounded me for the last ten years. I mistakenly assumed he was one of them, there to buy me, but my body knew he was different. My body went electric in his presence.

He's my electric yes.

I reach up and touch his face. "Darius." His eyes burn bright, blazing with his animal side.

He lowers his mouth in a ferocious kiss. He pries my lips apart with his tongue as his hips settle in the cradle of my legs.

I reach for the tie of the sweatpants to unknot it. I manage to get it undone and shove the waistband of the sweats down the curves of my hips.

"Paloma," Darius rasps. "I don't know if I should–"

"You should. We're okay," I murmur. "We're okay."

"It's not safe," Darius insists between desperate kisses. "I'm not safe. Being here with you on this mountain..." He rips open the flannel shirt I'm wearing, popping all the buttons. He's better than a Viking. He's glorious.

"You see? I'm out of control." He rents the fabric of my pink satin cami in half.

My exposed breasts bounce out, nipples taut.

He lowers his mouth, like he's desperate to get his lips over my nipple. He sucks hard, and I cry out, the answering tug between my legs making the flesh tighten there.

"Sorry." He lifts his head, breathless. "Was it too much?"

I grasp his ears and guide his head to my other nipple. "No. Keep going."

He swirls his tongue around it. Scrapes his teeth.

The suave, controlling lover from the beach house is gone. I thought nothing could top him, but it turns out, there was something even better.

Because I *love* Darius unhinged.

This rough passion is the magic that creates legends.

"I'm sorry." Darius is still apologizing for his animal side. His rough hands tug me down on the bed, so he can nip at my neck. I sense his internal struggle, guess that he doesn't like to be this way. To show this side of himself.

Finally, his brother said when he changed form.

Perhaps he's rejected this side of himself. Exchanged it for the manicured Wall Street Hedge Fund manager. He's at odds with the two sides of himself.

"No...no!" He roars, shaking his head so hard his neck cracks and snaps. My sense is that he's not talking to me– he's talking to his other half.

He's talking to the bear.

"I'm sorry, Paloma. I shouldn't be here with you. Not like this."

"You *should.*" I'm firm. I know from working with horses that if I follow his lead with fear, his animal will react. I have to maintain the energy of trust. Show him I'm unafraid. That we're friends.

"It's just that I'm not myself here. The mountain brings out my bear. And my brothers bring him out. And *you.* Especially you, princess. The moment I saw you back at Lockepoint, my bear went nuts. He's crazy over you."

"I love your bear," I assure him.

I don't know why I say it–I barely met his bear, but I can tell there's some kind of terrible struggle within Darius right now. I want him to feel safe being his true self with me.

Whatever that may be.

"I don't want him to hurt you."

I don't know how dangerous his bear is, but I do know his twin, who had an equally ferocious-looking bear, ducked his head when I hit him with a stick and then ran off when I told him to go. And I know his twin also assured me that Darius wouldn't harm me.

It seemed that Darius' bear only came out because Teddy goaded him into a rage, and that rage was about his insult to me.

"You won't hurt me." I run my hands over his bare shoulders, my palms loving the sculpted landscape of his bunched muscles. His hard cock finds the notch between my legs, and he groans, dropping his forehead to mine as he slides it over my slickness.

"Paloma..." He sounds broken. "I can't. I'm afraid I will mark you."

"Mark me? What does that mean?"

"A bear..." He groans as if he's in pain. As if being so near me is a torture.

I roll my hips beneath him, getting more contact with his shaft.

"Oh fuck," he groans.

"What does it mean?" I prompt again.

"Right. It's... a bear marks his mate with his scent." He scraps his teeth along the side of my neck. "Then other shifters know she's been claimed. My bear wants to claim you with his teeth."

His words give me pause, and I might have pulled back or slowed down, but at that same moment, the head of Darius' cock finds my entrance. I moan as my soaked sex parts for him, as if my body knows and understands I am his to claim.

I tip my pelvis and push back against the steady pressure of the head of his cock. I take in the tip. It feels delicious.

He groans in return. "I can't–" But his body doesn't obey his will. He penetrates me with one snap of his hips.

I cry out at the pain-pleasure. At being pried open by his thickness. Filled by his length.

"I'm sorry. Sorry, Paloma. I didn't mean to."

I know he's not wearing a condom, but I don't care. I'm taking charge of my own breeding, now, too.

Fuck Thom Thompson and all his sick plans for me.

"*I* meant to." I hold his gaze.

It turns steadier as he rocks into me.

"No biting," I say firmly, since that sounded dangerous. "But I want your Viking bear cock."

More of Darius returns, expression clearing from anguish and delirium to the sexy man who seduced me in my bedroom. His lips turn up at the edges.

He rides me, his beautiful body rocking over mine. "You want this, princess? You want this big cock?"

"Yes. This is what I want."

"You like it when I fill you up? When I stretch your sweet virgin flesh to take me?"

I smile like a satisfied cat as he makes the bed shake with his thrusts. "Not a virgin anymore," I brag.

Because I'm damn proud of taking control of my sex life. Of asking for and getting what I need. Of ruining all of Thom's plans for me.

"No, you're not, are you?" Darius braces one hand beside my head, using the other to keep my head from hitting the headboard. "You're mine now," he declares.

The rebel in me wants to deny it. I may like to pretend I'm the fair maiden captured by the Viking, but in real life, I belong to no one. Never again will a man hold me against my will.

Except Darius isn't holding me against his will. I want to be here, underneath him. I want to be the one driving him and his bear mad. I want him to claim me as his. Even to mark me with his scent, so all other shifters know.

I want to claim Darius Medvedev right back.

"You're mine now," I say back to him.

A slow smile spreads across his face, and he thrusts with intention. Like he's staking his claim on my pussy. On my womb. "That's right, little dove. I'm yours. You want this cock, you demand it. Morning, noon, or night–it's yours."

It feels so good that my eyes are rolling back in my head. I want nothing more than to be filled by this beautiful man-bear. Except, then it's not enough. I need more. Faster.

"Please," I start to chant. "Please...now. I need it."

"You need to come, sweetheart?" Darius' voice is rough.

"Yes. Together."

"You want us to come together?"

I want it. I may be inexperienced with sex, but romance novels have been my only form of entertainment for the past ten years. I'm programmed to believe in that holy grail of completion–the simultaneous orgasm where fireworks go off and volcanos erupt.

I want to reach the apex with Darius. I want us to be in this together. Because I suddenly have the sense that it's the only way we will succeed against Thom. Love is the oldest magic.

Thom separated me from Wren to keep us from using it against him, but he didn't count on Darius. The man whose bear knew we belonged together.

And I have the sense that together, we'll be unstoppable.

"Fuck," Darius mutters. "I'm losing control."

"No biting," I remind him, gasping at the force he's pounding me with. "Now, Darius! Please!"

Darius' face contorts. His beard seems to grow before

my eyes. He gives a shout and then bucks into me, the bed slamming against the wall so loudly, I suspect all seven of his brothers will hear it.

"Yes!" I shriek. "Yes!" I catapult off the edge, tumbling and spinning into oblivion.

There aren't fireworks. It's an avalanche. A cascade of pleasure that turns me inside out. And also a volcano–that's Darius, erupting and spewing his hot seed into me. So hot and copious, I swear I feel it hitting the back wall of my channel.

Afterward, it's the eye of a hurricane. The whipping winds of a storm all around us, but we're in the center, floating.

Cocooned in the still point of togetherness.

* * *

Darius

"Paloma," I croak, as reality seeps back in, and I realize what I've done.

I didn't bite her. At least, I don't think I did.

But I was out of control.

Fate, I *could've* bitten her. If I ever lost control of my bear around her, I could inflict serious damage. Hell, I could even end her life.

It's enough reason to break this thing off completely when we've defeated Thompson.

Never. My bear roars to the surface.

I roll off Paloma before I do something I regret.

She gasps at my sudden withdrawal.

I stand beside the bed where my feet landed, my gaze drawn to my cum smeared between her legs. "Fuck, Paloma. I lost control. I didn't use protection."

"I know," she says, calm as a cucumber. Are cucumbers calm? No, they're cool. Well, she's cool as a cucumber, then.

Agony over my mistake rolls over me. "I'll get you a washcloth." I head to the bathroom and get a warm cloth as she calls, "It's okay."

When I return, I find Paloma trailing her fingertips through my essence, using it to stroke herself, painting it all over her inner lips and clit, like she relishes being coated in my scent. Like she's marking herself human-style.

I nearly lose it again, my bear tearing at the leash, dying to sink his sharp teeth into her delicate human flesh. I freeze halfway across the room to her, breathing deeply through my nostrils to force my bear back down.

Paloma watches me with heavy lids, still stroking, as if she gets off on torturing me this way.

"Fuck, I want you," I mutter when it's safe to walk again.

"You have me," she purrs.

"It's not enough." I'm suddenly upon her, spreading those knees wide and using my tongue to help her distribute my essence over every millimeter of her sex.

She orgasms against my mouth, as if she was just waiting for my tongue to bring her to the finish line a second time.

I use the washcloth to clean her up, and kiss the apex of her slit, sliding my tongue in the cleft one more time.

She shivers and convulses again with another aftershock.

"You're a bear," she croons softly when I lift my head. She reaches for me, pulling my head up to her face for another kiss. "And what's going on with your hair? Does being a bear make it grow super fast?"

"Oh." I run my hand through my hair and find I have

Fabio-length locks. "Maybe my bear thinks if I look like a Viking, I can claim you."

Paloma's laugh is warm and husky. She kisses me. "I have a million questions."

"Yeah?" I settle beside her, tugging her to face me, so I can tuck her in close.

"Uh huh." She scrapes her fingernails lightly through the hair on my chest. "How often do you turn into a bear? Is it a full moon thing? Or an anger thing?"

I shake my head. "Not a full moon thing. Yes, anger." My hand finds her ass and squeezes. "And lust. But only with you."

She looks up at me from under her lashes. "No one else?"

"Never. My bear never wanted anyone else."

I watch the pulse at her throat quicken. She doesn't seem afraid–that's a relief.

"And to answer your question–almost never. My bear isn't safe."

"What do you mean?"

I shake my head. "I can't let him out because...he rampages. I can't control him when he's out. It's not normal–the rest of my brothers have control. It's...there's something wrong with me."

Paloma seems to chew on that. My psychic knowing tells me it's not true. Darius may not trust his bear, but the energy doesn't read that there's anything wrong with him. I let it go for the moment.

"Was the bear outside this window earlier Teddy?"

"No, that was Everest. Another brother. You met him on the rugby field."

"Right the '*pet*'." She makes little quotation marks in the air with her fingers. "So, all your brothers are bears?"

"Yes."

"Is your mother a bear?"

"Winnie? Yes. She's...in hibernation."

"Really?" Paloma sits up in bed.

"Yeah."

"Do you hibernate?"

"No. It's not really... normal. I mean, it's not abnormal, either. But we don't know why she's been asleep for years."

"*Years?* Is it like a coma? Is she on life-support? How does she stay alive?"

"Nah, she just nonstop sleeps. Occasionally she gets up, bathes, eats a little and then goes back to sleep."

Paloma reaches for my hand and covers it. "I'm sorry. That must be hard for all of you."

"Yeah."

"What's the deal with Teddy? Seems like you guys don't get along. What's that about?"

"He's just pissed off that I moved to New York to live amongst humans."

Paloma waits for more, forcing me to examine my words. "That's not really true," I admit. "He's pissed off because I wanted to develop part of Bad Bear Mountain in order to save it from other developers."

Paloma's eyes round. "Oh. I guess any development would be upsetting if you were a bear."

I slump under her assessment. "Yeah. I just thought if I could control the way it happened, at least we'd be able to salvage our side of the mountain."

"So what happened?"

"Teddy met Lana, his mate, when she was out here hiking, and her stepbrother tried to murder her. He rescued her. And then she rescued him right back. Turns out she's a billionaire. She's a clothing designer. She owns a plus-sized athleisure wear company."

"GoddessWear?"

"Yes, that's the one. So she saved the mountain from all development." There's a bitter taste of failure in that story for me, despite it all working out. I hate that I'm the bad guy when all I tried to do was make things right for our mom. For my family.

As if Paloma reads my mind, she squeezes my hand again. "You were trying to help, and they still blamed you. That must hurt."

I nod. Fuck. "Yeah. This...thanks. I've never talked about my family with anyone. It's a...uh, vulnerable place, to be honest."

Paloma's gaze is warm and open. There's a river of understanding flowing from her to me, despite the guilt and darkness I've felt over it all. "Hey, you know I come from the most fucked-up 'family' of all time." She makes finger quotes again when she says the word *family*. "I can tell you guys love each other. At least you aren't poisoning each other or locking people in towers."

I draw her face against my chest and kiss the top of her head.

"They think I'm greedy. And it's true—I went to New York to figure out how to get rich. My goal was always to save the mountain. But it took a lot longer than the younger me expected."

"But you did it. I heard Thom mention you had the fastest-growing hedge fund last year. He seemed proud, like he somehow had something to do with your success."

"He likes to pretend he mentored me," I scoff.

"Yeah, he takes the fatherly thing to a sickening level."

"The truth is...I believed I was going to save the mountain. I believed it right until last year when it no longer needed saving. And then..."

"It must be hard when your motivation for success falls out from underneath you."

My eyes inexplicably burn. "Actually...it made me realize it had all been a lie."

Paloma's forehead wrinkles in confusion.

Suddenly, I need to get it all out–the source of all my pain. The reason I fled to New York. The *real* reason, not the one I concocted to justify staying away.

"Teddy doesn't just hate me because I wanted to develop the mountain. He has deeper reasons."

Paloma waits again, but I find it hard to speak. She touches my shoulder. "You can tell me. Whatever it is–it's in the past. I won't judge."

I draw in a deep breath and try to explain. "I hit puberty early–really early. We were only seven when I had my first shift, and it was completely out of control. I was terrified. I knew we were bears, but our mom–our bio mom– never shifted. She didn't like to. She said she couldn't because we lived in this human trailer park.

"I didn't know what being a bear really meant. Or what it felt like to shift. One minute, I was seven years old, and the next, I was a scared cub trapped in a tiny trailer home. I had none of my human thoughts. I didn't know where I was. I didn't recognize the trailer. I didn't even know that the human woman and child in the trailer with me were my mom and brother.

"I just had the sense I was in the wrong place, and I needed to get out into the woods. Of course, I didn't know how to open the door or even what a door was. So I slammed around in the little trailer we lived in, tearing it all to hell trying to get out.

"I hurt my mom in the process. I slashed my claws across her chest and face. I stabbed Teddy. Finally, Teddy opened the door, and I raced out."

"God, Darius. I can't imagine how traumatic that was for you."

"I just remember blind terror. I didn't know what had happened, or how to shift back to human form. My mom didn't follow. She could have shifted to give me a mama bear who could help me, but she didn't. Winnie, our adopted mom, would have. She knew how to raise young bears."

"Why didn't she?"

"I don't know. It was like our real mom was afraid of bears, even though she was one."

"What happened to you?"

"I ran. I found my way into the woods, and I kept running for three days and nights until I finally collapsed in exhaustion and changed back to my human form.

"It was Winnie who found me–up here on Bad Bear Mountain. She found me and eventually located my mom and brought me back to the trailer. Three days later, our mom dropped us off at Winnie's house and disappeared forever."

"*What?*" Paloma's eyes are wide with shock. "She abandoned her children?"

I try and fail to swallow past the lump in my throat. "Yeah. Basically. She left a note to Winnie that said she didn't know how to raise bears."

"God, that must've been confusing and heartbreaking for a little kid."

It helps to have her name the trauma for me. I internalized the whole event as my bear being out of control. Terrorizing me and my family. Causing wounds that can't be healed.

That's what I'm afraid he'll do with Paloma.

Sometimes I forget that I was just a tiny kid. It's no wonder I couldn't handle my bear.

"So maybe Teddy hates me for that—I don't know. Winnie was patient, but my bear continued to be out of control for years. After high school, he enlisted in the army, and I went to New York. We've been on completely different paths ever since."

I'm looking out the window, so the salty scent of Paloma's tears takes me by surprise. My head whips back to look at her. Her beautiful brown eyes swim with tears, and she's wiping more away underneath them.

"Oh fuck." I sit up and tug her onto my lap, leaning against me. "Don't be sad for me."

"I'm sad for both of us," Paloma says. "We have both been tragically apart from our siblings for far too long."

"I don't know about *tragically*," I mutter.

"Yes, the tragedy is you two could've worked it out long ago, but you were running from yourself. And you made that self out to be Teddy."

I stare at Paloma, my heart thundering unnaturally in my chest. If anyone else had said it, I would've ignored them. Walked away, like I always do. Suppressed any feelings that caused me pain, just as I suppress my bear.

But it's Paloma. My *mate*. The female who already holds my heart. The female I want to give everything to.

"I don't know if I was running from myself. But definitely from my past. I wanted to go somewhere my bear couldn't hurt anyone. Away from this mountain where I could barely control him."

"It sounds like you're afraid of your bear. Maybe you got that from your mother."

"It's no wonder my mom was afraid–my bear *hurt* my mom. And she's a shifter, so she healed, but if he did something like that to you–"

"I mean she was afraid of her own bear."

I swallow the torrent of damning words that were about to flow out of my mouth about my bear and the damage he's done.

I blink.

It never occurred to me that my mom was afraid of *her own* bear.

And I sure as fuck don't want to be like my mom.

But...fuck. I did the same exact thing she did! I abandoned my family because they were too bear-like for me to handle.

Right now, I wish Teddy were here beating the shit out of me. It would feel so much better than the deep shame that's burying me alive.

"Fuck, you're right," I mutter, rubbing my forehead.

"Come on." Paloma climbs off the bed and tugs my hand. "Let's get you cleaned up–you still have the forest on you, and I could use a shower myself."

I follow her to the bathroom and turn on the shower, and I then treat Paloma to a slow, sudsy round two.

Chapter Ten

Paloma

The shower is amazing, in more ways than one, but even better is the sense that Darius and I have connected on a new, deeper level.

He's more than the insanely hot Viking warrior. More, even, than a man who can change at will into a bear.

He's human. Or at least, my definition of human–a man with a heart that hurts.

As I put on another one of Darius' flannels, a knock sounds at the door. "Yoo hoo! Darius? Paloma?" a female voice calls from the front of the cabin.

"That will be Lana." Darius pulls on a pair of jeans and heads, shirtless, to answer the door. I follow in nothing but his shirt.

A curvy woman with smooth, dark skin and long, pink-tipped braids throws her arms around Darius' neck. Behind her, Teddy stands awkwardly holding two large shopping bags.

"Darius! How dare you come to the mountain and not

come to say hello," Lana mock punches him, making her braids swing. Her hair is the same soft pink as her jumpsuit.

"We were coming to say hello," Darius grumbles, receiving her hug with a warm embrace, "but your mate decided to knock down a tree and challenge me to a fight in front of Paloma."

"Yes, I heard about that." Lana pulls away and glances affectionately over her shoulder at Teddy. "He's very protective of the cub." She turns her attention to me, reaching for both my hands instead of shaking one. "And you must be Paloma. It's so nice to meet you. I'm so thrilled to have a sister-in-law. How are you feeling? I heard about the poison—how horrifying!"

"Um, better, thanks."

Lana is a lot to take in, but I instantly love her. I've been lonely as hell for far too long, especially missing my sister, so I don't mind that she's already adopted me as her new kin.

"Good. Matthias can heal anyone—even of poison. Here, I brought some clothes for you." She turns and takes the shopping bags out of Teddy's hands. "I didn't know your size, so if you like anything here, and it doesn't fit, we can run to my clothing outlet in town."

Teddy still hasn't said a word to Darius yet—the two just glower at each other behind our backs.

I take the shopping bags she thrusts at me and peek inside.

"Come on, I'll show you what I brought." Lana guides me toward the bedroom. "We'll see if the two grumps can bear-hug and make up."

I flash her a grin. "I see what you did there."

Her smile back is dazzling. "Bear jokes have to be your jam when your mate's name is Teddy."

"Teddy!" I laugh as we enter the bedroom and shut the

door. "*Teddy bear*. I don't know why I hadn't put that together yet!"

"It's adorbs, right? And all the cabins have this *Goldilocks and the Three Bears* vibe going. I love it, but we built something bigger, so we could start a family." She puts her hand on her round belly.

"Yes, I heard. Congratulations." I dump the contents of both shopping bags out on the bed. "How far along are you?"

"Fourteen weeks." Lana sorts through the clothes, unfolding and holding them up with a narrowed eye like she's gauging my size. "Thank you. Teddy was already super protective, but now he's going insane with it. I'm sorry if he made you feel unwelcome." She tosses a three-pack of panties at me. I rip them open and pull on a pair under the long shirt.

"That's definitely not the case. I think he was just goading Darius to find out if you're his fated mate. But now that he knows you are, he'll protect you like family. You *are* family."

Part of me wants to reject all this insta-family stuff. I have a family–Wren. And I have to get to her before Thom does something horrible. But it also feels easy. Comfortable.

So different from being trapped in the gray stone tower of Lockepoint.

Out in the cabin, I hear Darius' voice, but it sounds like he's on the phone, rather than working things out with his brother.

Lana thrusts a pair of black stretchy yoga pants with wide legs. "These might work. They can double as dress pants with a pair of heels. Deep pockets. Very versatile. Good for travel."

"Sold." I tug them on. They are high-waisted with a wide band that controls and flatters my tummy.

"They look best with a crop top. Here, I think this will fit you." She hands me a bright melon sports bra with fancy straps that converge in a ring in the center of the back, extending out like spokes. "This is my most comfortable sports bra line, and then you can layer over this midriff jogger." She gives me a long-sleeved teal crop top with a wide neck and thumb-holes on the sleeves.

Everything fits perfectly and feels like it's made of the highest-quality fabric and construction.

"I love this, thank you."

"Oh good. At least you have something to wear until you can shop for yourself. We can head down to my outlet shop in town if you want to look for some other things."

The sound of the front door opening and heavy boots clomping into the cabin interrupts our conversation.

"That will be...everyone." Lana flicks her brows at me with a grin. "Now that you're firmly in the category of fated mate, the whole family is going to want to get to know you."

"I really can't stay." The underlying anxiety about getting to Wren is growing louder. My gut says I'm running out of time. "I need to get back to the East Coast and get my sister."

Lana's expression turns to concern. "I understand. Let's go see if they've found anything out about where she is."

When we emerge from the bedroom, all of Darius' brothers are present. They're all so giant, they can't all fit in the living room. Axel and Bern stick their heads in from the window. A bear–the same one they called their 'pet'–lurks outside the open front door.

Darius extends an arm to me, and I go to his side. Already we're a couple. Part of me wants to resist it because it seems so fantastical, so impossible, but it also feels exactly right.

He tucks me against him and kisses the top of my head. My resistance melts even more.

"Paloma, you've met Matthias, Axel, Canyon, Bern, and Hutch. This asshole is my brother, Theodore." He lifts his chin at Teddy. "You weren't formally introduced since Teddy was busy making you feel unwelcome."

"Sorry about that, Paloma." Teddy speaks in the same deep rumble as Darius. "You are more than welcome. You're family—marked or not."

"That's Everest there." Darius indicates the bear.

I wave nervously at the giant animal, trying to imagine what he might look like in man-form.

"Paloma is anxious to get back to the East Coast to find her sister," Lana offers.

I send her a grateful look. She definitely has my back, and I appreciate that.

"Yes, have you heard anything?"

"That's why I called everyone here," Darius says. "We located her. The choir tour is on their final leg in New York. We found out the hotel they're in, and we have friends en route to get her out. They should be there within the hour. Even though they block internet access, Kylie was able to hack into her school laptop and link her to a satellite. As soon as she opens it, we can connect you through my phone, so you can let her know what's going on."

I let out an exhale in an audible gust. "Thank God! Thank God." Tears smart my eyes. "I'm so glad you found her."

"We will leave immediately to rendezvous with her. Brothers..." Darius breaks off as if it's hard for him to ask for help.

"We'll go if you need us," Matthias says.

Darius lets out his own exhale. "Thank you. I trust the wolves, but I would rather have my brothers there."

"Bear power." Bern pumps his fist in the air.

Darius' phone beeps, and he whips it out of his pocket to look at the screen. "This is it." The tautness in his voice tells me what it's about.

I grab his wrist to bring the face of the phone closer to me.

On it, a young woman in her early thirties appears. She doesn't take time to introduce herself, she just speaks as she clacks keys on her keyboard. "Wren is online. I'm patching you through right now." The screen goes black, and I hold my breath for one second. Two. Four and five. Then suddenly a video comes on.

Wren stares at the screen. She looks surprised. "What's this? Oh–*Paloma!*" Her face breaks in to a giant grin. "Oh my God! How did you connect us? I missed you on Sunday. What happened? Where have you been?"

"Listen, Wren. There's no time to talk. Thom wants to kill you."

I hate to scare her this way. I spent years trying to shield her from Thom's evil, but I have to arm her with knowledge now. "He murdered our parents, and he's been poisoning me for years to make me think I was sick."

"*What?*" Wren's face drains of color.

"He's been holding your safety over my head to make me work for him, but I got away. We have friends on the way to get you out of there within the hour. Pack a bag now, so you're ready when they show up."

Just then, the door behind Wren bursts open. Wren screams. So do I.

Men dressed head to toe in black and carrying assault rifles spill into the hotel room.

"Please tell me these are your friends?" Wren asks with wide eyes.

I look to Darius, unsure, but the answer becomes clear when Thom leisurely walks in behind the group chomping on a cigar and carrying some kind of baton.

"Hello, Wren."

I want to smack the smug smile right from his face. "Ah, perfect—there's your lovely sister. And Darius, my poorly-behaved guest. Just the people I hoped to find."

His men grab Wren and wrestle her away from the screen.

"Stop it!" I scream. "Get them off her."

"Now, now," Thom mock-soothes me. He points the baton at Wren and some kind of taser shock issues from it.

"No!" I scream as my sister slumps to the floor.

"Quiet, Paloma. You can't throw a tantrum when I clearly warned you what would happen if you tried to run away again."

I scream at Darius's phone. "Let her go!"

Of course, he won't let her go. I'm being irrational. I need to get my wits back, so I can outsmart this maniac.

I suck in a deep breath and then another, but there's no room to let in more air. Oh yeah, I forgot to exhale. I blow my breath out, slowly.

Thom settles into Wren's chair and surveys me with a satisfied smirk.

I'm going to kill him.

"Now, here's what's going to happen. You're going to return to Lockepoint with your new friend Darius, or Wren won't live through the night."

"I'll come," I say in a hurry. "I'll come—just leave Darius out of this."

Thom's smile broadens. "No, no, my dear. Darius is a part of it now. The only thing that will save Wren's life is both of you coming together. I want you there by midnight."

Darius takes the phone from me and holds it up to his face. His eyes glow amber with rage. "We can't make it by midnight," he snarls. "We're on the other side of the country. But I can get us there by morning—six a.m."

"That will be too late." Thom laughs, as if he will delight in murdering a young girl. He probably will.

"Four a.m.," Darius bargains. "That's the best we can do. Even with a private jet, the flight will take almost five hours."

"Drop a pin to your location to prove to me where you are."

"No!" Teddy roars.

Thom—the sick bastard—smiles enough to show teeth. It's disgusting. "Who is there with you, Darius? Family members?"

Darius growls, "If you want Paloma, you'll have to wait till four a.m." He ends the call before Thom can reply.

"What if he doesn't?" Fear crawls up my throat.

"He'll wait. If he hurts Wren, he loses his leverage over you, and you're far too valuable an asset for him to give up."

Teddy growls. His eyes are the same shade of amber as his brother's.

I look around and realize all eight of the brothers' eyes glow. The entire room hums with low bear growls.

"Let's move." Matthias stands.

"What?" I ask. I'm shaking, still in shock over seeing Thom tase Wren. "Where are you going?"

"We're going to help you," Teddy says. His voice is deep and thick, more bear than human.

I rub my face. I have to think, to figure out what to do about Wren, but my thoughts are spiraling. Darius puts his hand on my back, and the weight steadies me. "You can't...I can't ask you to do that." I know they said they'd help get Wren, but now they'll be facing off with Thom and all his guards. "It's going to be dangerous."

"We love danger," the triplets chorus.

"You're with Darius," Matthias says. "That makes you family."

I don't know what to say. I can only gaze at them all, emotion clogging my throat.

The big bear pokes his head through the door and grunts. It would be scary, except I know he's Darius' brother, and the expression on the furry face is so earnest.

"He says 'don't worry,'" Axel interprets.

I have the strongest urge to pet the bear's head, but I'm not sure if that's polite. So I nod, swiping my angry tears.

"We're going to get Wren back," Darius says. He wraps me in his powerful arms, and I let myself sink into his hug.

"That's right," Hutch says as Darius' brothers crowd around me, offering their comfort. "They're about to find out that you don't mess with the bears."

Chapter Eleven

P*aloma*

My stomach was in knots the entire flight back east. Darius let me use a laptop on the flight, and I used it to set up my own leverage against Thom.

Now, as we fly the short distance from New York City to Lockepoint, I'm a complete disaster. It's horrible to return after trying to escape it for so many years, but even more horrific is imagining all the dastardly things Thom might do to Wren if we don't get there in time.

I blink back tears. *No, I can't think about it.*

Darius squeezes my hand. We're in the back of a repurposed military plane. Matthias sits on my opposite side, checking through his first aid kit.

The comms unit crackles with the pilot's announcement. The sound is loud but unintelligible.

"We're approaching Lockepoint now," Teddy interprets. He's sitting a few feet away from Darius, next to his ex-military friends from Taos. They are also shifters. They used to all be on a shifter special ops team with the military, but now they have a private security firm.

"Is it weird being back here with us instead of flying this thing?" the Taos guy asks Teddy.

Teddy shrugs. "Buddy flies just fine. I trained him myself."

I look from Teddy to Darius. I don't think they've had time to talk out their disagreement. They've just agreed to put it aside to help me rescue Wren.

All the Bad Bear brothers are on the mission. Five of them are flying in on helicopters, while Darius, Teddy, and Matthias are with me. Teddy's special forces buddies are here, too, the ones who operate as Black Wolf Security out of Taos. They brought the plane.

"How did you even get all this equipment?" I motion around the plane. A sleek boat made of gray metal takes up most of the space.

"Friends in high places," Darius says.

"More like friends in low places." The Taos guy leans out to grin at me. I've noticed he's kind of a flirt. I think his name is Lance. His white teeth shine out of his camo-painted face.

Teddy, Matthias, Darius, and I aren't in any war paint, just military-grade combat gear. I'm wearing a bulletproof vest that's a heavy leaden weight on my shoulders. A necessity, since I'm the only non-shifter here. The four Black Wolf Security guys are in high-tech gear and bodysuits that will allow them to strike a target hard and fast in the dark.

A few days ago, I didn't know shifters existed. Now they're risking it all to help me rescue Wren. It's overwhelming. I've gone from being locked alone in a tower and used for my gifts to surrounded by new friends who don't know or care that I have a weird intuition that results in profitable stock trades.

The Black Wolf Security leader, a tall, dark-haired guy

named Rafe, marches around the boat to stand in front of us. He's got a calm, focused presence that inspires confidence. A lot like Matthias.

"We're ready. We'll drop the boat. Then you four" –he points at me, Darius, Matthias and Teddy– "parachute down to meet it. Buddy's going to drop the rest of us closer to the beach. We'll make a hole and cover you, so you can head straight to the mansion."

I try to imagine each of these steps, but all I can picture is a jumble of every action movie I've ever seen.

"Got it?" Rafe finishes the debrief. I have the feeling he's repeating the plan for the civilians. My mouth is dry, but I nod.

Teddy rises, grabs three parachute packs, and helps Matthias and Darius strap into theirs. "Paloma, you're with Darius."

My heart is trying to pound out of my chest, but I stand so Darius can strap me to him. My wild heartbeat calms as I lean against him and soak in his warmth.

"You two lovebirds have fun," Lance says.

Darius growls, but I raise a hand and flip Lance off.

Matthias chuckles. One of the Black Wolf guys barks a laugh. Lance slaps a hand to his heart, pretending to be wounded.

Rafe shakes his head. "Serves you right, brother." To me, he says, "Welcome to the team."

A buzzer sounds, and I nearly jump out of my skin. I grip the side pockets on Darius' flak jacket. We're face to face, and I've never been more grateful for his huge Viking build. "I've got you, little princess," he rumbles. "I mean, warrior princess." He bows his head, so he can brush his lips against mine.

"Awww," Lance and another Black Wolf security guy chorus. "Kiss cam!"

Both Darius and I flip them off without even breaking the kiss. He smiles against my mouth, and I find enough breath to chuckle. I had no idea members of a special ops team could be so goofy.

Then Rafe gives a signal, and the back of the plane opens up. The wind howls a few feet away from me and Darius. Adrenaline pumps through me. I pull down a pair of night goggles and secure them.

Darius tightens his grip on me.

Rafe gives a thumbs up. A mechanism triggers, deploying a grayish-white parachute. It flies out first, a bright circle in a dark night. The boat follows.

Rafe and the rest of his team walk to the plane's center. They've attached themselves to straps to approach the opening without getting blown out.

Teddy strolls past them and, without hesitation, leaps into the night. At first, his legs seem to fly up, and then he's hurtling down after the boat.

Matthias tucks his glasses in a pocket, zips it shut, and saunters to the end of the plane. He lets himself fall, his limbs spread-eagled in the howling wind.

It's Darius and my turn next. My stomach flip-flops as we approach the dark maw of freezing air.

"Let's do this," I shout. And then the wind steals the breath from my mouth.

Darius and I fall, hurtling towards the roiling ocean.

There's a jerk as Darius deploys his parachute. I brace against him and blink rapidly to clear my watering eyes as we float more gently downwards. The plane roars overhead, heading toward the distant strip of sand.

Beyond the beach, Lockepoint mansion glows. Every

window on every floor is illuminated. It's beautiful and pathetically unguarded.

Thom's hubris will be his downfall.

The plane swings low. Against the bright lights of Lockepoint, I can see four dark shapes leap out of its belly. They each hit the water with a small splash.

"They don't have parachutes." I suck in a breath.

"They don't need them. They're shifters. They can hit the water and survive," Darius murmurs. "They'll take the beach and clear a way for us to land the boat."

The wind whips my hair over my face. We float closer to the water. I brace myself to hit it. Some of us don't like swimming in November.

I glance down. "Look." I tug Darius' vest to get his attention.

Below us, Teddy and Matthias have gotten into the boat. Teddy's at the controls, driving it towards us.

"Perfect timing." Darius fiddles with some mechanism on his parachute and lets us drift slightly to the right. Teddy steers the boat under us. Matthias stands, ready to grab us. Both he and Teddy are dripping wet.

"Hang on." Darius releases the parachute, and we fall a short distance. I grit my teeth to keep from crying out.

Darius' feet hit the metal hull with a bang. Somehow, he keeps his balance as the boat rocks on the choppy water. That must be another perk of being a shifter.

Darius unstraps and checks me over while Teddy points the boat toward shore. My legs wobble like jelly, but I grab Darius and hold on to stay upright.

The next thing I know, Darius clutches me to him and pulls me down to the floor of the boat where he can bend over me, covering me with his body. My ears ring–there's a crack, crack, crack in the distance and a rat-a-tat-tat of answering machine gun fire.

"They're storming the beach." Teddy slows the boat, and the wind dies.

"Should we help them?" I ask from my cramped position under Darius.

"Nah, they're good. Wait for the signal."

I slap Darius' arm. "You can let me up."

"She's wearing a vest," Matthias says. "Remember?"

"Sorry." Darius helps me upright. His eyes are brightly lit. "Protecting you is my number one priority."

"Here." Matthias hands him a black matte helmet. Darius helps me put it on. I agreed to wear this headpiece because it's bulletproof, but it must be state-of-the-art. The glass face plate gives me night vision. The world glows green, and I can see the yellow-white shapes of the team's heat signatures in the distance. I watch with fascination as they slip up the dunes, each descending on a guard house. There are soft booms up and down the sandy strip as they set off charges and then move with whiplike speed to take out any guards that survive the guardhouse explosion.

"We need to get closer, so we're ready," Matthias says. Through the helmet, the sound of their voices is amplified while the crack of bullets seems muted.

"On it." Teddy motors us closer. "Just wait for it."

"Wait for what?" My own voice echoes in the helmet, but the twins hear me just fine. Back at the mountain, Hutch told me shifters have heightened hearing, and can see in the dark. I'm beginning to understand why special ops is a natural career choice for shifters.

"Wait for the distraction," Teddy says.

A loud whistling sound goes up, and firecrackers burst in the sky beyond Lockepoint.

"There it is." Matthias grins. "Courtesy of a few more of our friends from Arizona. They snuck up from the road."

More firecrackers explode, showering the sky with rainbow colors.

Two helicopters appear from the east and west. They fly up to the house from opposite directions and pause to hover over the gables. A rope lowers from each bird, and two dark figures shimmy down to the roof.

I can't be sure, but I think one of them is wearing a kilt.

"Axel and Canyon," Darius murmurs.

One of the helicopters tilts sideways, and a huge shape leaps out onto the steep roof of my old bedroom tower. It rises to hind legs and waves a paw at the helicopter pilots as they zoom away.

"Is that...?"

"Yes, that's Everest," Matthias tells me. "He's the final stage of the aerial attack."

The bear falls to all fours and lets out an echoing roar.

Teddy's busy gunning the engine. "Brace yourselves," he snarls. The boat skims the water, pointed straight towards the beach.

Every muscle in me tenses, expecting a crash when the boat rams the shore. Instead, Darius grabs me, crouches, and leaps, just as the boat plows into the beach.

He and Matthias land side by side. Instantly, two black-clad figures–their body heat turning them bright gold through my helmet–flank us. It's Lance and Rafe.

"Let's move," Rafe says. He and Lance hold guns and hunch low to cover us as we run up the beach. I let Darius swing me into his arms. He can run faster than I can, and we need to get to Wren.

In seconds, we're at a set of side doors. Matthias kicks

them down, and Rafe and Lance step in first, swinging their guns to check the area beyond.

"Clear," they shout and race on. We move through the house, with Rafe and Lance clearing each room before Darius, Matthias, and I walk through.

The place is eerily quiet. The sight lights on the guns sweep over the marble floors. The priceless paintings on the wall are silent witnesses to our invasion.

"West wing," I say. "Thom will have Wren there, in the panic room. And there'll be lots of security."

"Not anymore," someone calls. Canyon strides around the corner, stopping short when he sees the gun sights trained on his bare chest. "We tore into the roof, took out a couple dozen guys at once. Everest threw a bunch of them out of the windows. What's the word for that?"

"Defenestrated." Axel appears behind Canyon. He's eating what looks like an apple. "The way to the west wing is clear."

"Let's go." I step forward. "This way."

Darius and his brothers all fall in around me. "The safe room is in the lower levels. There'll be more guards down there."

"We'll take care of them," Matthias rumbles, his eyes shining with an eerie blue light. "It's time to show them just how bad our bears can be."

Chapter Twelve

*D*arius

We march down the hall. I try to stay one step ahead of Paloma, so I can take a bullet for her, but she's leading us.

Behind me, there's the sound of crinkling plastic. Axel has finished his apple and is eating something else. Corn chips, by the smell of them.

"How can you eat at a time like this?" Lance asks him.

Axel shrugs.

"He always has snacks," Canyon says. "Did you bring me any?"

"Nope." Axel tips the bag upside down to pour the last crumbs into his mouth.

"Focus," Matthias orders. I'm glad he's with us. He's one of the few people, other than our mother, who can keep Axel and the triplets in line.

I have bigger things to worry about.

I can feel him. My bear. He's trying to explode out of my skin.

Not now, I tell him.

Mate. The bear shoves an image of me in bear form holding Paloma. *Keep her safe.*

I am. I grind my teeth, forcing my bear to surrender. The last thing I need right now is to lose control of the bear. I need my wits about me.

We've reached the corridor where Axel and Canyon took out a bunch of guards. Bodies lie everywhere. Blood smears the wall where they were thrown against the wall. Bloody paw prints lead up the stairs. Everest was here.

"Down this way," Paloma tells us. She stands back and lets Rafe and Lance lead us down the first flight of stairs. "The largest safe room is on the subterranean level."

With every step we take, the tension grows.

We reach a locked door with a black keypad and a sensor used for a fingerprint scan.

"Let me try." Paloma steps up and puts her hand to it, but it flashes red.

"Plan B," Rafe says. He punches the wall, ripping out the keypad entirely. Metal bars come down, but we rush to grab them. Everyone but Paloma joins in. It takes all our strength, but we bend the metal and make a hole so we can claw out the entire steel frame of the door.

The passageway beyond is dark, except for flashing orange lights.

"No use for stealth. They know we're here," Rafe shouts. He and Lance rush into the breach. Matthias and I are next, on either side of Paloma. Axel and Canyon bring up the rear.

We have Paloma in the middle to protect her. A shifter wall to take the brunt of an attack.

It's a good thing we do because three seconds later, we run into more guards.

* * *

Paloma

Shots sound and someone roars in pain. In a flash, I'm pressed up to the wall, covered by Darius. I peer past his arm.

The helmet turns the hallway an eerie green. Golden shapes dart to and fro. Lance and Rafe crouch to return fire. The werebear brothers run forward to take out the shooters.

I happen to look back the way we came. "Look out," I scream. Another wave of guards pours down the stairs.

Axel and Canyon turn back, and nets shoot out. They land on the younger werebears, the mesh glinting in the flashing lights. Canyon screams, writhing.

Darius cusses.

"Go." I push at him. I wish I had a weapon, so I could help. Instead, I hunker down to create a smaller target, and Darius charges into the fray.

For a moment, there's nothing but gunfire, screams and roars. I crawl on my hands and knees to the closest were-bear–Axel. The net is unusually heavy, like a fishing net made of metal, but I manage to lift a corner up. He gasps, wriggling out from underneath it. Both of us crawl to free Canyon. He cries out as we drag the net off, and lies there, shuddering. The lights flash, revealing his bare torso. It's crisscrossed with red lines, like he's been burned.

"What happened?" I ask Axel.

"Silver," he answers. His own face has red marks where the net landed on his bare skin. "The net is poison to shifters."

My blood turns icy cold. The new guards have weapons that hurt shifters. "But...that means..."

The lights power up completely. I'm blinded for a second until my helmet adjusts.

Darius, Matthias, Rafe and Lance stand over the bodies piled on either side of us. "They know what we are," Rafe rasps. "And they know how to take us down."

"No," I breathe. This is a nightmare. These shifters are risking everything to help me, and now their lives are in danger, too.

A comms unit crackles. Rafe and Lance put their fingers to their earpieces at the same time.

"Report from the outside. More of Thompson's troops have arrived," Lance says. "Deke and Channing are pinned down."

"Tell them they've got silver nets," Matthias says. He's crouched beside Canyon and Axel, checking their wounds.

"I'll be fine," Canyon croaks. His body is crisscrossed with red marks. He got the worst of it because he wasn't wearing a shirt. Axel just has marks on his arms and face. Matthias and Axel get Canyon up between them.

"You don't have time for this." Canyon pushes Matthias away. He leans into Axel, and they both stagger but stay upright.

"We need to keep going to get Wren," Axel says. His eyes blaze green.

"No, you're injured. Bear form, now," Matthias orders. "You'll heal faster."

"But—" Canyon protests.

"Now," Matthias growls. His voice booms and echoes like he's in an amphitheater. Goosebumps break out on my arms.

Canyon and Axel respond to Matthias' order. They fall to all fours with their backs hunched. A second later, they're in bear form.

156

"Go," Matthias commands. "Get Everest and get out any way you can." He waits until they lumber off to turn to Rafe and Lance. "You need to go, too. Cover my brothers, and then reinforce your team."

"Are you sure?" Rafe asks.

"We got this," Darius rumbles. He turns, and I follow, stumbling over the fallen net. He steadies me. Matthias takes up the rear. Rafe and Lance have disappeared.

We come to the round vault-like door at the end of the hall. The safe room. There are no more guards, but no way in.

This last part is up to me.

I pull off my helmet. The cool air hits my sweaty temples. "Thom," I shout. "You wanted me to come back. I'm here."

Chapter Thirteen

P*aloma*

Nothing happens. Thom doesn't respond to my challenge. My heart sinks.

Darius and Matthias step forward. "We can try to break in."

"No," I say. "The entire chamber is made of steel."

Matthias holds up a hand. His nails have become bear claws. "We can try." His voice is thick, like his vocal chords have begun to change.

"He's got Wren." I shake my head. "If we try anything, he'll hurt her. But the one he really wants is me."

There's a hissing sound, and I step back automatically. The vault door slowly opens, revealing Thom. He's got my sister propped against him. Her eyes are closed.

He's holding a needle with a syringe of clear liquid to her throat. "You're late," he informs me.

I raise my hands, to show I'm not armed. "You don't want her. You want me." I take a step forward.

"*Paloma.*" Darius steps in front of me.

A huge man steps out from the shadows behind Thom.

He's holding an oddly shaped gun with a giant barrel. He fires two blasts back to back.

I flinch, but Darius takes the hit. He falls, half covering me. I stagger under his weight, and we both sag to the floor.

A few feet away, Matthias slams against the wall. He tears at his shoulder, which is bloody. He's been hit. He groans and slides down the wall, leaving a bloody smear. His head falls back, and his eyes close.

Darius groans and pushes off me. His side is bloody, but he's still able to move. The bullet must have clipped him.

I scramble out from under him. He braces his hands on the floor, veins in his face popping.

"Get...away..." he tells me. His eyes are pools of fire. His teeth elongate, growing until they don't fit his jaw. His bear is about to break free.

I scramble backwards, just in time to clear the space for Thom's henchman to deploy a silver net.

Darius roars loud enough to deafen me. He's pinned under the net, his body writhing. His bones pop and grind as his bear fights him.

Thom's henchman raises the shotgun.

"No!" I lunge, stepping in front of the barrel. "Don't hurt them." Making sure I keep my body between Darius and the shotgun, I face Thom. "It's me you want. Take me. Just don't hurt them."

"She's right. She's the money. Take her," Thom tells the huge man.

The man prowls forward, moving with that predatory grace that I've noticed in the other shifters. His eyes are pitch black. Like a demon from a nightmare.

Thom leaves Wren's side. She slumps to the floor, her head lolling on her neck.

"Wren," I shout. The big guy grabs me. I twist, trying to

break his grip, but it might as well be an iron shackle. His hand is so large, it wraps around my arm.

Thom's at the back of the safe room, keying something into a keypad.

"What's wrong with my sister?" I snarl at him. "What did you do?"

"I told you, you were too late," he says. The keypad beeps, and a door swings open, leading to a musty smelling tunnel. "I already injected her. But sadly, we won't be able to wait around to watch her die."

"No," I scream. Under the net, Darius roars. Thom ducks into the escape tunnel, motioning for his henchman to follow. I plant my feet, but am helpless as the brute drags me away.

* * *

Darius

I'm pinned. All my strength is going to fight the bear. My spine cracks as he tries to take over. The wound in my side doesn't help. The bullet only grazed me, but it was silver. I'm bleeding, and the silver poison is making my bear feral. I'm losing control.

I can only watch as Thom and his guard–some kind of shifter–drag Paloma through a second vault door. It closes and hisses as it locks. I'm left alone with my fallen brother and Paloma's sister.

No. Get her now, my bear thrashes. If I shift now, the silver will burn every part of my bear's body. I have to keep him down.

Matthias groans beside me. He's been hit by a silver bullet. I can tell by his extreme weakness that the slug is still inside him. I need to free myself from the net, so I can help him.

"Matthias? Darius?" Teddy roars from the opposite end of the hall. He charges up to us, holding a machine gun in hand. He's in a black bodysuit made of a special material that his shifter ops team wears on missions. It conforms to their bodies even when they shift. Blood smears his face and beard. The fighting on the beach must have been bad.

"Here," I shout.

Stopping to rip the flak vest off a fallen guard, he wraps his hands to protect them before grabbing the silver net and pulling it off me. I rise, choking on adrenaline, and he whips around to crouch by Matthias.

"What happened?" Teddy asks.

"Thom's bodyguard shot Matthias. Took Paloma."

I clench my fists, bracing against the bear. My nails have grown to claws, and they shred my palms.

Let me OUT, the bear snarls.

Never, I reply.

Teddy frowns at me, but turns back to steady Matthais against the wall. He's alive, his canines elongated as his bear fights the poison.

"Shoulder," Matthias gasps. "Silver bullet."

Teddy raises his hand, his nails elongating to claws. He scratches at Matthias' shoulder. Matthias roars loud enough to shake the walls as Teddy digs the bullet out.

I win the fight with my bear and rise to go to Wren. She's lying slumped on the floor, her eyes closed, her face pale. I put a hand to her throat, feeling for a pulse.

It's there, but it's faint.

"No," I pant. "No..." I've failed Paloma.

I've failed Wren. I've failed everything.

Teddy helps Matthias to his feet. Matthias limps to me.

"It's too late," I say. "He injected her...just like he said he would."

"Pick her up." Matthais kneels beside me. His shoulder is a bloody mess, but he looks determined. He opens his vest and pulls out a carefully rolled fabric case that contains a number of vials. He holds one up and readies a syringe. "Get her upright."

Teddy reacts first, kneeling and carefully sliding a hand under Wren so he can sit her up.

I cradle her head. "It's okay, Wren. We're Paloma's friends."

She mumbles something, but doesn't open her eyes. She looks so much like Paloma, with the same heart-shaped face and dark hair. She's thinner, and fine-boned like the bird she's named for. Her body weight is as light as a handful of feathers.

"Extend her arm," Matthias orders. He's deep in doctor mode. Or maybe it's Alpha mode. He certainly used alpha command when he spoke to Axel and Canyon.

He swabs Wren's arm with antiseptic. Her limb looks tiny and fragile in comparison to his large hand.

"Wren, listen to me." His voice is deep and soothing. "You're going to be okay. I have the antidote." He preps the syringe and checks it for air bubbles.

"What is that?" I ask. The liquid is clear, but my shifter sight detects the faintest pink tinge.

"A special cocktail I created myself. It includes a cure-all donated by a vampire friend."

Vampire blood can heal humans.

I watch Matthias inject the blood and bow my head over Wren. Even my bear is quiet, hoping it will work.

The dead silence is broken by her high-pitched gasp.

"Her heart's beating stronger." Matthias rises, folding up his medicine kit. "But we need to get her out of here."

I rise with Wren in my arms. "I need to go after Paloma."

Teddy turns. "Then this door needs to go." His eyes flash, and he tears into the wall beside the vault door. He rips out chunks of drywall and hits a rock wall. He doesn't stop trying to worry the stone, clawing around the rounded steel door to pop it free.

"I'll take her." Matthias holds out his arms. I carefully lay Wren in them, and he cradles her against his unwounded shoulder.

I turn and help Teddy claw into the wall. His body grows, muscles swelling into the fur-covered bulk of the bear. With his bear power, he rips the door out of the wall.

My twin faces me as the bear. *Go*, he seems to say. *Get your mate.*

"Keep Wren safe." I clap him on the shoulder before racing down the dank tunnel.

I can hear Teddy turn to lumber after Matthias. They'll get Wren out. I trust them.

I'm halfway down the tunnel when I get a hit of Paloma's scent.

And then I have to brace against the mold covered wall to fight my bear from bursting forth.

Let me out. It's my turn now, my bear demands.

"No." I grit my fangs and almost fall to my knees. "No." *We're wasting time!*

There's fresh air wafting towards me. I'm almost to the end of the tunnel. I fight the bear every step of the way, my spine hunched and muscles straining. I emerge doubled over.

Thompson's forces are waiting for me. A flurry of darts

164

hit my body. I pull one out, snarling, and the silver tip burns my fingers. I toss it away and brush at the rest of the darts, but my bloodstream is on fire. I take a step, and a wave of weakness overtakes me. My limbs turn leaden, and I stumble.

A silver net knocks me down to the ground, and the poison in my veins drags me into darkness.

Chapter Fourteen

Darius

I swim in a sea of pain. Shouts and screams sound in the distance, then I hear the clank of bars slamming down.

I come to again when a soft hand closes around mine. I jerk and Paloma shushes me. "Shhh, Darius. I'm here."

"Princess?" I slit open my eyes, but the world is blurry. My head aches like someone pounded it with a sledgehammer.

"Oh, thank God you're awake." Paloma's soft hair falls on my cheek, and I turn my head to drink in her sweet scent.

My skin burns where the net touched it, but the pain is nothing to the fire raging inside me. Whatever was in those darts is poison. I feel incredibly weak.

"Where–"

"They took us somewhere. I overheard one of the guards say we're on a private estate, but I don't know where. They drugged me. They drugged us both." Her breath hitches. She's been crying.

I want to raise a hand to comfort her, but I can't lift it more than a few inches. She grabs it and holds on with both hands.

There's something important I have to tell her. I reach through the fog to find it.

"Wren," I mumble.

"I know," Paloma's voice cracks with a sob. "Thom poisoned her. I can still sense her, but she must be dead..."

"No. Matthias. Medicine." My lips feel heavy, but I force them to shape the words. "She...alive."

"*Ay, Dios mio,*" Paloma gasps. "Oh, thank you." She presses my hand to her face. I feel the rain of her tears.

"It's okay."

"We're going to get out of this. I promise."

"I wouldn't be too sure about that," someone rasps. A sharp, clove smell hits me. A heavy thump of boots brings the scent closer. "Give him another dose of tranq. He's awake."

"Stop," Paloma snaps. "What are you doing?" She drops my hand, and I sense her standing, defending me. "Leave him alone!"

My chest rumbles as my bear voices his wrath. There's a whoosh and another dart pricks my chest.

"It's just a knockout drug," the guy rasps. "Special blend for shifters. It'll burn but there's not enough silver in there to kill him."

I hear Paloma fighting, and my bear pushes to the surface, making me surge upwards. But the dart has done its work, pumping the tranquilizer into me. I'm fading.

A heavy hand lands on my chest, pushing me down with laughable ease. I choke on the numbing scent of cloves. "Rest up, bear man. We'll have use for you later."

* * *

Paloma

I watch as Darius' body goes limp. The guy standing over him has to be some sort of shifter. He's huge, with a scarred face. Big, black sunglasses hide his demon eyes.

He sets down the crossbow he used to shoot Darius and faces me. "Mr. Thompson wants to see you."

I fold my arms over my chest. "If you think I'm going to do anything he says, you can think again." Now that I know for sure Wren is alive, all my emotions have turned to rage.

"Suit yourself," he shrugs. "I'm not the one with a boy bear whose life is on the line."

"What are you going to do with him?" I ask, in case he'll gloat and give me more information. I don't know much about our situation. Thom's men gave me a tranquilizer to knock me out. I woke up here, in this cold hangar with a concrete floor, lying on a medical table next to Darius. He's restrained in silver chains, but they're letting me move about freely. For now.

The big guard doesn't answer. The door at the end of the large space bangs open, and Thom trots in, followed by a group of guards.

"Paloma," he shouts in his reedy voice. "What have you done?"

I move, so I'm standing between him and Darius. Thom stomps over to me. He's supposed to be intimidating with his angry face and the armed guards. But I feel no fear, nothing but hatred. This man kept me and my sister captive. He tried to murder my sister and almost succeeded. He had his troops try to kill my friends.

He deserves what's coming to him and more.

"You wicked child," he says. His normally pale skin flushes an unhealthy red. "How dare you target my fund!"

I know why he's so upset. He's discovered the trades I made on the flight over here. I spent the whole time making trades that would ensure the downfall of Thompson Capital. I know exactly what Thompson's holdings are, and how to target them.

"What's wrong, Thom?" I taunt. "Did someone boost the profits of the companies you were shorting? After a bunch of those deals go through, you'll get caught...shall we say...*short*."

"You bitch."

"Careful." I examine my nails. "You'll give yourself another heart attack. It's only a few hundred billion."

"You'll find a way to make it back. Every penny. Or else—"

"Or else what? You'll kill an innocent child? I'm done with your threats. You can kill me. But then it'll be all over. You'll have nothing. You'll be nothing. Because that's what you're really worth, right? You inherited a fortune, and in a single decade, you ran your family's companies into the ground."

"You shut your mouth—" He steps forward to strike me, and I slap his hand away. He's not used to me being able to fight back.

"You know it's the truth. The only thing you've done was kill my parents and take me and Wren prisoner, so I'd build your fortune. And with a few clicks of a mouse, I took it all away. You're a failure. And the world will know."

"You will rebuild all you've taken from me. I will chain you here, and you will never see the sun—"

"I will *never* work for you again." I use my rage as a weapon. I've never felt so much power with Thom—I was

170

too trapped in his web before. Now that Darius got me free, I'm a new person.

He sputters, unable to speak.

A phone rings, cutting him off. He pulls out his cell and stiffens when he sees the name on the screen.

"Is that one of your investor friends?" I ask. He turns beet red, so I know I must be right. "They can't be happy with how much money you've lost them."

"Oh, they'll be happy." He pockets the phone. He's breathing heavily, but a tinge of triumph enters his voice. "Because not only will you rebuild my investments, you'll rebuild theirs. And I have something else to offer them." He points to Darius. "A shifter to hunt."

I suck in a breath, feeling like he punched me in the gut. My skin crawls at his smile. Terror seeps back in, bleeding me of the rage and power I felt a moment ago.

"You wouldn't."

He chuckles, feeling like he has the upper hand. "Something you never knew about me, daughter. I'm part of an exclusive club. We call ourselves the Venatores. It's an old Latin word that means *hunters*. And guess what sort of creature we like to hunt?"

"*No*," I croak. I don't want to believe this, but it makes sense. The silver chains, the nets, the tranquilizer: Thom's men were prepared to take shifters down. There was a reason he told me to bring Darius back with me, and it wasn't for revenge.

He is so sick.

"Oh yes. Ordinary game is no longer a challenge. That's the reason I invited Darius to Lockepoint in the first place. To confirm what Hannibal here had already sniffed out." He motions to the big, scarred guard.

Hannibal is huge. He has to be another shifter, one who

turned on his own kind. Because who could better teach someone how to hunt a shifter than another shifter? He'd know all of a shifter's strengths and weaknesses.

Thom cocks his head to the side. "Do you think Darius' brothers will come to save him if we put up the distress signal?"

Ice water floods my veins at the thought of the werebear brothers storming in to save Darius and me, only to be captured, one by one. "No," I croak. "You can't."

"Oh, I'm going to. Darius will be the first to be hunted as soon as he calls on his friends."

"He won't do it."

"I think he will." Thom motions, and a guard steps up, opening a medical case and showing me the vials inside. "Especially if I threaten to poison you. That's one thing I've learned about shifters. They'll do anything if you threaten their fated mate."

* * *

Wren

"Are you sure you want to do this?" the doctor, Matthias, asks. He's seated beside the bed in the guest room where I'm staying. Beyond him, the huge blond guy, Teddy, and his gorgeous wife Lana stand in the doorway. Matthias and Teddy are my sister's friends, and they rescued me. Apparently, I was on death's door after Thom poisoned me. Luckily, Matthias was there and able to heal me.

Right now, I feel amazing. I'm riding a surge of energy, and instead of lying down to rest, I want to do anything I can do to help find and rescue Paloma.

"I'm sure." I lie down and close my eyes before anyone can argue. Connecting psychically with my sister is easy as breathing. Right now, my rescuers are doing all they can to find her and her boyfriend Darius. Thom took them, and no one knows where. I can use my psychic gifts to See where they are and maybe get some clues to their location.

I calm my breathing, like Paloma taught me, and slip into a trance. Next thing I know, I'm looking down at the version of myself lying in bed. Matthias waits beside me, head bowed in thought. Teddy paces the living room of his and Lana's gorgeous mountain home. Lana is watching him worriedly.

I let myself sink deeper, and the vision fades. I expand my energetic field, imagining a ball of light pulsing bigger and bigger until it's stretching from horizon to horizon. My sister is out there, and I can sense her energy–it's so much like mine.

All of a sudden, she's right next to me. I touch my energy to hers, but she's too preoccupied. Her field is full of worry and a heavy sadness. I imagine light and love flowing from my heart space into hers.

The picture of where she is becomes clearer. I keep feeding Paloma my warmth and let the vision solidify.

She sits in a big warehouse type place, with boxes and guards all around. Next to her is Darius. I take in every detail of her surroundings, trying to get a clue as to where she might be.

"They're in a warehouse in a forested area. Somewhere high in altitude," I murmur.

"Good, that's good. They're both alive? What else?" Teddy asks.

"Thom is there. I...don't see him, but I can sense him. Blech."

Wren? Paloma senses me nearby but can't see me. I

173

send a push of love her way. She's still worried and confused, but she accepts my presence.

Satisfied, I turn to Darius. His energy is a raw, pulsing wound, and I can't ignore it any longer. He's in so much pain.

I drop to my knees beside him, trying to send healing energy. I only sense more rage.

And then the light changes, and I get a vision of Darius not as a man, but as a huge brown bear.

"There's a bear inside Darius. I don't know—that's how it shows up."

"That's right, Wren. Darius has a bear side, and if he would let it out, it could save them. Can you tell him to let it out?" Teddy asks.

I study Darius. There's something over him, isolating him from me and everyone, even Paloma.

The shadow over him solidifies into dark bars. Darius' bear is in a cage.

I pace closer, and an angry paw swipes out, narrowly missing me. I jump back. The bear roars, a wounded, echoing sound.

"I know," I tell it. "You're not free." I pace around the structure, but it's solid. I can't figure out how to break it open. The bear won't let me get close enough to comfort him.

I need someone to speak to the bear and calm him down. He doesn't trust me. Who would he trust?

All at once, I'm back in my body in the guest bedroom.

I open my eyes and sit straight up, startling the others in the room. Matthias, Lana, and Teddy all peer at me.

"Are you all right?" Matthias leans in to check my vitals, and I hold up a hand. I don't want him to touch me. I'm about to try something I've never done.

If it works, it could change everything. But if I fail, I could lose my sister.

It has to work.

I turn to Teddy. "I need your help."

* * *

Darius

There are murmurs all around me. I strain to hear, but my ears fill with the bear's roaring.

And then it all fades, and I hear Teddy calling my name. "Darius."

I see him clearly, striding out of the darkness towards me.

"Brother? What's happening?" The darkness dissipates. We're both standing in a forest clearing. I recognize every rock and tree. "This is where we grew up."

Am I dying? Is this what people mean when they say their life flashes before their eyes?

"We need to talk," Teddy says. "There's something I need to tell you."

"I don't have time for this. I have to get back to Paloma. She needs me." I can feel the pain in the distance. Terrible things are happening while I'm asleep.

"She needs you." He takes a step forward. "But you need your bear."

"What?"

"Brother, listen." He stares into my eyes. It's like looking in a mirror, or would be if he shaved his bushy beard. "Embrace your bear."

"I can't." I shake my head, retreating. "I can't let him out."

"You can. You must."

"No. He's too wild." I turn around, and there it is, the trailer where we lived. The one that I destroyed. Its side is dented in. "He'll ruin everything."

"He can help. He can save you."

"No. He can only cause destruction." I can feel the hair growing on my chin, sprouting into a beard like Teddy's. Maybe that's why I shaved, to keep from looking too much like my twin. To keep from looking wild.

All for nothing. My bear is trying to break out.

"Look at this." I wave a hand at our ruined trailer. "Look at what he did."

"You have to embrace that side of yourself. You have to be who you were meant to be."

"And Paloma? What if he hurts her? What if he scares her?"

"She's strong, She won't scare easily."

"She'll leave," I shout.

He comes closer, and I push him away. "Like Winnie. Like mom."

"No–" Teddy grabs me, wrapping his huge arms around me. Somehow, the bastard is stronger than me. I try to fight him, but he just holds me.

He holds me until I stop my struggle.

"She left because of me," I say, and as the words leave my mouth, I hear them in a smaller, younger voice. I've shrunk to the size I used to be when I was young.

Teddy crouches to the level of my shorter self. "It wasn't your fault our mother left. You can't blame yourself." He morphs and becomes younger Teddy. No tattoos, no beard. A mirror image of me.

"It wasn't about us," he says in his seven-year-old voice. "She made her own choices."

"I'm all alone." The clearing has grown dark.

"No, brother. I never left you." Teddy throws his skinny, seven-year-old arms around me. "I never have, and I never will."

And then we're grown again, back in our adult bodies. "Neither will our brothers. We're not going to leave you."

The clearing has faded, and our childhood trailer is gone, replaced by the cabin on Bad Bear Mountain. My cabin. The home I rejected.

"Neither will Paloma. But she needs you now."

There's a shadow lurking behind the cabin. It's too big to hide behind the cabin, so it hulks there, its spine bowed. Its eyes glow, and the light glints off its oversized claws.

It's a monster, scary enough to give a child a lifetime of nightmares.

"He's waiting. He's your strength. You have to let him out."

I say nothing. I don't even have the energy to tell him "I can't."

Teddy studies my face and sighs. "This is my fault. I was wild, just like you. I fought with you too much. I didn't realize it then, but I was trying to provoke you to embrace your bear. If I'd realized that sooner, I could've done a better job and just talked it out instead of fighting."

I glare at him. "This is my dream, and you're making it about you?"

"This isn't a dream. And your mate needs you." The light flares in his eyes, and I see his own bear looking back at me. "You're out of time. Remember what I told you."

He steps back, bunching his fists. I recognize his stance well. He's about to start a fight.

I raise my hands. "Wait–"

He knocks my defenses away and socks me right in the face.

* * *

Teddy

I wake with a gasp, flailing. Something's trying to strangle me, and I let out my claws to tear it to pieces.

"Teddy," Lana calls. She's right next to me. "It's okay."

I force myself to stop fighting, feeling wild. I'm in the living room in our new mountain home, lying on our leather couch. Lana's beside me, sitting on an ottoman. Matthias is standing behind her.

Shreds of baby blue fabric litter my chest and the floor.

I brush them off. "What...?"

"It was a blanket covering you," Matthias says. "You destroyed it."

I sit up and rub my face with both hands. "Sorry."

"It's okay." Lana holds out a hand and waits for me to take it. I pull her into a hug, needing her solid warmth to ground me.

After a long embrace, she pulls back and lets Matthias check me over. He must be satisfied with my vitals because he leaves and goes into my guest bedroom, quietly closing the door.

"Did it work?" Lana asks. "Did you make a connection?"

"I think so. I don't know." The trance state put me into a dream that was so real. "I saw Darius, spoke to him. I think he got the message."

I rise to my feet, unable to sit any longer. My knuckles throb like I've punched someone. Darius has just a hard head in a vision as he does in real life.

The door to our guest room swings open, and Matthias walks back out, escorting Paloma's sister Wren. She looks pale and shaky, and I rush to help her sit down.

"Did it work?" I ask. "Did you reach them?"

"It worked." Wren says. Matthias helps her sink to the couch.

"Give her some space," he orders.

Lana tucks a blanket over her shoulders. I jog to the fridge to get her a glass of water.

Matthias holds it, so Wren can drink. After a moment, the color returns to her cheeks, and she clears her throat. "They're alive. I can sense them both."

"Did you get any impression of where they were?" Matthias asks.

She nods. "In a steel frame building, like where you keep a small plane. I sensed a lot of land around them. Forest. Some mountains. There was a stack of boxes with a logo on them. A circle around an X. Both the circle and X were made of silver chains."

"Got it," Matthias rises and pulls out his phone. "I'll let Kylie know. She's tracking all private plane flights in the US. This will help her pinpoint where Thompson could've taken them." He heads outside to make his calls.

"You did good," I tell Wren. "Thank you."

She nods. "I linked you and Darius, so you could give him the message."

Goosebumps rise on my arms. I don't know how these psychic visions work, but when I stood there with Darius beside our childhood home, it all felt real.

"I gave him the message," I say.

"Then it's done." Wren blinks and lifts her head. Her eyes have a dreamy quality. "Now it's up to him."

* * *

Darius

179

I come to, thrashing awake. I can't move much. I'm upright and bound to a hard surface by heavy chains.

I'm in the same space as before, surrounded by guards. Thom and Paloma stand a few feet away.

"Darius." Paloma strides towards me, but two guards grab her and pull her back. "Let go of me."

"Paloma," I growl. I don't like anyone touching her. Neither does my bear. He lurks under my skin, but doesn't fight to come out.

I remember my dream—the dream that Teddy told me wasn't a dream. It felt so real. My face throbs from where Teddy hit me. The pain is good and clean and invigorating compared to the sickening weakness the silver brings.

In my dream, my bear was a misshapen monster.

Embrace the bear, Teddy told me.

"Tell him," Thompson says to Paloma. "Tell him what we plan to do to him and all his shifter friends."

"Let me go, and I will," she says. He motions to the guards to let her go.

Paloma walks slowly toward me. "Darius, I need to tell you something." She steps close to me. Her beautiful face is solemn. "I don't know if we're going to get out of this. But it doesn't matter. The only thing that matters is..." she takes a big, shuddering breath. "I love you. I will always love you."

"Princess," I whisper. I strain in my bonds, wishing I could break free and hold her.

"Whatever happens, I want you to know that." And she whirls and snatches up the crossbow that was sitting on a nearby table. She faces the crowd of Thompson's men. "If you're going to hurt him, you're going to have to go through me."

"No." A big guy in black sunglasses pushes his way through his fellow guards. He smells weird, like he's covered in clove oil. I can't get anything else from his scent. He bears down on Paloma, who stands firm, expertly bracing the crossbow against her. Guarding me as I should be guarding her

"Don't hurt her," Thompson cries. The big guy slows his approach, and Paloma shoots him in the chest. He roars, ripping out the dart, but the tranquilizer is designed to work quickly. The weakness overtakes him, and his legs bow, causing him to slump.

"Who's next?" Paloma bares her teeth. She looks like the warrior princess she is.

Ever since we first met, she called me her Viking. Because that's who she needed me to be. She didn't need the civilized man in a suit. She needed a warrior. Someone strong and wild, who would stop at nothing to fight for her.

She has no idea how wild I can be. It's time I answer the call and bring out my bear.

I need you, I tell him. *Our mate needs you.*

Mate?

We will mark her. But first, we must break free.

I give up control, and it's like taking a breath of fresh air after holding it for years. My lungs fill. My muscles swell. The bear pumps strength into my body, more than I thought possible. The silver under my skin burns like acid, but I lean into the pain.

My arms and torso tingle with excruciating sensation. Metallic droplets bead on my skin, tinged with red. I'm sweating silver. Silver and blood. I blink, and silver tears run down my face, leaving trails of fire.

The weakness leaves my body along with the silver. All that's left is to break the chains.

Paloma is still waving the crossbow, providing a distraction.

"Don't just stand there. Grab her," Thompson orders his men. They run forward. Paloma shoots another dart, but is quickly overwhelmed. They grab her and bring her to Thompson.

"Hold her. I'll administer the injection." He plucks a vial of blue liquid from a medical case and holds it up. I can smell the acidic stench from here.

Poison, my bear shouts.

Save her, I tell him. He hesitates. I've fought him for so long.

I'm sorry. I was wrong to subdue you. You are a part of me, and I need you. You are my strength.

He rises to his feet. Energy pumps through me. I strain in the chains. They don't budge, but the solid metal at my back buckles.

"No," Paloma tenses her arms, leans into the men holding her and kicks her legs in Thompson's direction. More guards rush to grab her legs.

"Hold her still," Thompson orders. He advances on her, ready with a syringe of poison in his hand.

I bow my back, bending the metal around me. The chains loosen enough that my feet can touch the ground. I can stand, with the metal table at my back.

"Wha–?" The guards nearest me hears the clank of chains and turns.

And I let out my bear.

* * *

Paloma

A roar shakes the walls and the concrete floor. Thom jumps and drops the syringe he was about to inject me with.

"What?" he looks annoyed, turning to see what's interrupted him.

A guard goes flying past us, and crashes into a knot of six other guards. They fall like bowling pins.

Darius is on his feet, still chained to the metal slab, but somehow able to move. He drags the whole apparatus with him. The chains clunk as he stomps towards the rest of the guards.

"Shoot him," Thom screams. He tries to run and falls.

The guards whip out their guns and fire.

"No," I shout.

Darius whirls and the bullets hit the metal at his back. There's more creaking and popping sounds, and then a giant furry paw reaches up, grabs the top of the metal slab, and jerks it over its head.

Darius' bear stands up. The chains still bind his huge, furry body. There's smoke rising and a sizzling sound where the chains burn his flesh. But it doesn't seem to care. It drops to all fours, charging a line of guards so quickly, they don't have time to leap out of the way before he pounces on them. Guns and human arms go flying.

I let myself go limp in the guards' arms. They drop and abandon me to grab their guns, and I'm able to roll away.

More guards form a line to shoot at Darius, and I find the crossbow again. I take cover behind a fallen table, brace against the bow's recoil, and shoot at them. My aim is off, but it distracts them enough to turn and shoot at me while I duck.

Bear Darius' form flexes. His body grows impossibly huge. The silver links strain to the breaking point, and he bursts free from the chains.

More guards pour into the hangar.

"Look out," I shout.

Bear Darius doesn't need my warning. He's already rampaging around the room. Gripping the chains used to bind him, he whips them around. He becomes a hurricane of fur and silver chains that blows through the hangar, ripping through guards, knocking over equipment, and splintering stacks of boxes.

In the madness, the guards keep firing, but he keeps coming. The bullets only seem to make him madder. He roars loud enough to shake the building. His pelt is red with his blood, and the blood of his enemies.

Most of the guards have fallen, mowed under by the lethal whirlwind. A few run for the door, and the bear gives chase. There are wet, meaty sounds, and blood sprays. It's a massacre.

There's a groan nearby. The big shifter guy, Hannibal, is rousing. I rise with the crossbow, but can't find any more tranquilizer darts. They're lost in the chaos.

"Darius," I shout. "We have to go."

The bear whirls around. Its golden eyes fix on me, and I feel a ripple of fear. Is Darius there, behind that wild gaze?

"Darius," I keep my voice low and firm, like I'm talking to Starlight. "It's me. You've done well." I take a step, and my foot hits a patch of something slick. I keep walking, not daring to look down. "...but it's time to leave now. We can escape. Together."

Something grabs my leg, and I yelp, almost losing my balance. Thom has me.

I shake him off, but he hangs on. "Get off me," I growl.

A huge shadow falls over us both. The bear is right there, growling. The bits of brown fur that aren't matted with blood bristle.

It rears up on hind paws. *Dios*, it's twice as tall as Darius in human form. Goldilocks would shit her pants.

I want to call his name, but my mouth is too dry. I can only stare up at him.

With a giant, blood-encrusted paw, it gently nudges me out of the way. The heat of its body is like a furnace, searing me.

It drops to all fours, shoves its head near Thom's, and bares its teeth. Its mouth is big enough to swallow Thom's head whole.

I don't really want to see the bear eat someone, but I can't look away. The bear places a paw on Thom's chest, but doesn't press down.

Instead, its form morphs until Darius is standing there, human and gloriously naked. His fingers are fisted on Thom's collar.

"Paloma," Darius murmurs.

"I'm here." I make my way to his side. His wounds look worse on bare human skin, but even as I watch, the worst of the gashes and silver burns are closing.

"What do you want to do with him?" Darius asks me. His voice is gravelly.

"I have money," Thom says in a rush. "I'll give you anything you want–"

"You don't have money," I remind him. "Not anymore." My boot hits something small and sends it rolling. I stoop and lift the syringe he was going to use to inject me with poison.

I know exactly what I'm going to do with it.

"You kept me prisoner for years," I say to Thom. "You tried to kill Wren."

Thom twitches and opens his mouth. Darius' growl silences him.

"You were going to hunt my shifter friends for sport."

Darius sees what I'm intending, and rips open Thom's shirt, baring the old man's scrawny chest.

I crouch and tell Darius, "Hold him."

Thom writhes but Darius is too strong and grips the old man, so he can't budge.

"This is for my parents." I plunge the needle into Thom's chest. I don't know what dosage Thom prepared for me, but I can bet it's strong. He meant to punish me, weaken me. And he's had heart issues. "Let's give you a taste of your own medicine."

Thom's eyes roll up into his head. He starts thrashing. Darius releases him and lets Thom's limbs drum on the concrete floor. We both watch as he goes still.

I turn away from the sight of his body, feeling nothing. Thom deserved to die.

"You did it." Darius wraps his arms around me. I hug him gingerly and pull away.

"You're bleeding."

"It's worse that it looks. It's not all my blood."

"We have to get out of here. Can you run?"

"Yes. But you don't have to. Climb on." He steps back, and with a whole body shiver turns back into the bear.

I take a moment to run a hand down its fur. It's thick, and softer than I would've imagined. The bear grunts at me, and lifts an arm to boost me onto its back. I settle on top of it and take handfuls of the bear's fur, so I don't slide off.

There's a crash behind us, and Hannibal rises from the detritus of the warehouse. His glasses got knocked off, and his black eyes glint. He bares his teeth at me. His fangs are growing bigger before my eyes.

"Go," I shout and grip the bear's fur. Bear Darius lumbers towards the wall and tears a hole in the metal siding. I duck to shield my eyes from the falling debris. The bear's muscles bunch under my legs, and we shoot from the hangar into thick woods.

Riding a bear is nothing like riding a horse. I plaster myself to the bear's back as best I can, but his bulk is too broad for me to grip well with my knees. It doesn't help that we're racing over uneven terrain, dodging bushes and trees. Bear Darius keeps reaching back to push me into place.

I get the hang of it just in time for a roar to go up behind us. This roar is different from a bear roar. It's more like the bellow of a water buffalo. Something is crashing through the woods behind us. Trees are falling in its wake.

Hannibal is coming for us.

Bear Darius picks up speed. I flatten myself against him and squeeze his big bear neck. He's running flat out, but Hannibal is gaining on us. What I wouldn't give for a tranquilizer dart right about now.

A tall pine tree arcs through the air and crashes down beside us. Darius veers left to avoid it. A few seconds later, another.

Hannibal is herding us. But where? I can't lift my head very much without risking falling off.

Overhead, there's a *thunk, thunk, thunk* sound. I tense, expecting a new sort of attack, but a big black helicopter flies overhead. The wind from its propeller shakes the tops of trees.

Bear Darius runs through a boulder studded clearing, and the chopper swings down. Canyon sticks his head out the open side.

"Head this way," he shouts and waves his arm in a westerly direction.

There's a crunch nearby. Through the trees, Hannibal has uprooted a tree and is hoisting it to launch it at the chopper.

"Look out," I scream.

The tree trunk sails through the air, straight towards Canyon.

"Shiitake!" Canyon shrieks and ducks back inside.

"Hang on," shouts Bern from the pilot's seat. The chopper zooms off to the west. Bear Darius follows, leaping over boulders. I'm jostled so much, my legs go flying, only to bang back down on Darius' back. The only thing securing me are my arms around the bear's neck.

Ahead of us, the forest ends abruptly. I can't see until we break from the treeline to run over the rocky face. We're on top of a cliff. I can tell from the falling trees that Hannibal is right behind us. He has us cornered.

Bear Darius dashes forward. He's going to run us right off the cliff. I bury my face in its fur.

At the last second, the chopper swings out and dips low.

Bear Darius leaps–

Bern tips the chopper on its side–

Bear Darius grabs the skids. The chopper rocks wildly but doesn't plummet to the earth. We hang in the air. My arms strain, fighting to keep hold of Darius.

Hannibal skids to a stop on the cliff's edge and throws a final tree trunk like a spear. It hurtles through the air. Bear Darius twists to avoid it. And I lose my grip on his neck.

"Darius," I scream.

He shifts in midair and reaches out, grabbing my arm. The move jars my bones all the way up my shoulder, but I will him to hold on.

"I've got you," he says. His fingers wrap around my biceps, holding me tight. We dangle in the air, breathing hard, until Canyon reaches down to help us up, and Bern throttles the helicopter up and away.

Chapter Fifteen

Paloma

The minute we touch down on Bad Bear Mountain, Darius points to the small hangar on the side of the runway. "You've got a welcome committee."

There, standing next to Everest in bear form is Wren.

Darius, whose hair and beard grew Viking long again since he let out his bear, helps me out of the small plane. After the helicopter rescue, we switched to a puddle jumper. Bern did the flying and Canyon co-piloted. The two behaved rather competently.

As soon as my feet hit the blacktop, I run across the tarmac. Wren meets me half-way, and we collide into a big, messy hug.

"*Gracias por Dios. Gracias por Dios.* I thought you *died,* Rencita."

"*Estoy bien*—I'm okay. *Y tú?*" Wren weeps in my arms.

"No, I'm okay, too." We're both sobbing with joy.

"Where's Thom? What happened?"

"Thom's dead." I look over my shoulder at Darius, who stands behind me like he's still guarding my back.

"Your badass sister gave him a taste of his own medicine." Darius smiles at me.

"You killed him?"

"I injected him with the same poison he had waiting for me, but I guess he hadn't built up a tolerance to it, and you know, he had that heart condition." I shrug.

The big bear on the tarmac wanders closer. "I guess you've met Everest." I'm not sure how much Wren knows about the bears on Bad Bear Mountain, but there'll be time to figure all that out.

"Oh yes. He's been showing me around." She arches a brow at me. "I heard your boyfriend is a bear, too?"

"This is Darius." I disengage from her reluctantly, so she can shake Darius' hand. "He and his brothers saved our lives."

Wren ignores his outstretched hand and throws herself into his arms for a hug.

Darius gives a surprised chuckle before his arms lift and wrap around her. "It's nice to meet you, Wren."

"I'm not going back to school," Wren says fiercely when she emerges from Darius' arms.

"No, you're not," I agree. "From now on, we stick together. Unless, of course, it's time for you to move on and go to college and do the normal stuff young people are supposed to do."

"The normal stuff you weren't *allowed* to do," Wren says darkly. "I always knew something wasn't right, but you made it seem like it was all fine." She gives me a gentle shove. "Why didn't you *tell* me what was going on?"

"I just wanted to keep you safe and sheltered from his madness. If you knew, you would've insisted on sticking around, and then he would've found out that you have psychic abilities, too."

190

"Speaking of psychic abilities." Darius drops a hand on Wren's shoulder. "We heard you were responsible for figuring out where we were being held."

Wren smiles. "Nah, I just got clues. It was your hacker friend who figured out the rest. What did Teddy say her name was? Kylie?"

"Yes, Kylie."

"But I did connect you and Teddy, so he could tell you to let your bear out."

I turn to look at Darius, whose mouth drops open. "That really happened? I thought it was a hallucination."

Wren looks pleased with herself, as she should.

"Oh, yeah. Did I tell you that my talented sister has psychic skills, too?" I toss an arm around Wren's shoulders proudly. "She has a knack for showing up in my dreams. I didn't know she could psychically connect two other people."

"I never tried it before," Wren says. "But I'm sure it helped that you two are twins."

"I doubt that," Darius mutters. "We're not close."

Wren tilts her head as she studies him. "You felt very close to me. Almost like you didn't know where one of you stopped and the other began."

I make a soft, "mm" sound because that makes sense to me energetically. Darius has been at odds with his brother because he's been at odds with himself. With his own bear.

"Hop in, guys!" Lana waves from the passenger side of a shiny white Jaguar SUV that pulls up right beside us. Teddy is behind the wheel. Both of them climb out to embrace us as we climb into the back seat with Wren.

"Wren can stay at our place," Lana says. "We have her all situated there already, and you two probably need to rest and recover for a bit."

191

"And take care of some unfinished business," Teddy grumbles from the front seat.

Darius bares his teeth and growls back at him.

I laugh and grab Darius' giant biceps. "Is he talking about what I think he's talking about?"

"What is it?" Wren asks.

"He needs to butt out of my bear business," Darius declares.

I chuckle. Lana joins me. Even Teddy lets out a humored snort.

"Seems like Teddy might have been right about your bear business," I remind him.

Darius' face softens. "Yeah, brother. Thanks for the punch in the face. It was exactly what I needed."

* * *

Darius

Teddy and Lana drop us off, and I carry Paloma into my cabin, her lush legs wrapped around my waist, her hot core pressed just above where I want it to be.

"Princess, I'm gonna tear your clothes off so fast you're going to scream," I warn her, kicking my boots off in the entryway.

I feel my bear roaring up with excitement, but I'm not worried about him now.

I built my bear up to be something grotesque. Something dangerous. A monster who hurt the people I love. When I was on my rampage at the warehouse, I realized that while he is capable of those things, he is still me. The only reason my bear side was so wild when I was a child was because I wasn't old enough to understand how to be a bear. Puberty came too early, and our biological mom didn't offer me any understanding or training of what it meant or how to manage it. I couldn't control my animal side, and that scared me, which, of course, scared my bear and made him even more unpredictable and unsafe.

I rejected my animal side believing that gave me the control I desperately craved at that dark time of my life. Instead, it made my bear *more* out of control, more frustrated, and unable to seek fulfillment.

Rampaging in bear form to save my mate was infinitely satisfying. Nothing could come close to the feeling except marking Paloma.

She loops her arms around my neck as I stalk through the small cabin and nibbles on my ear. "Is that right?" she purrs. She wants me to make her scream. I think she wants me to mark her, but I have to make sure.

"Uh huh." I carry her into the bedroom and toss her on the bed.

"Do you know what happens now?" I use my gruff Viking voice with her, partly because I know she loves it and partly because my bear is out. I'm letting him shine through. His aggression is my aggression. My aggression, his.

"Are you going to mark me?" she asks.

I yank my shirt off without opening the buttons, causing them to fly in every direction.

Paloma giggles.

"That's right, beautiful." I prowl around the bed. "Is that all right with you?"

She smiles up at me. Her face flushes with desire, her eyes are bright, despite our ordeal. She nods.

"You're not afraid of my bear?"

Her laughter is thick and warm as honey. "Why would I be afraid of your bear? He just rescued me from death."

I climb over her.

"Also, Darius, he's *you*. He's not some separate entity you turn into. You *are* the bear."

I grin at her like the fool that I am. "That's exactly the conclusion I just reached, princess." I claim her mouth, kissing her thoroughly the way I intend to for the rest of my life. "Which proves you're the perfect female for me, not that I had any doubt." I continue to kiss her, rocking my rigid cock against the notch between her legs. "You're one person who understands me even better than I understand myself. Even more than Teddy—not that I'm admitting that asshole may have known me better than I did."

Paloma laughs. "There is one thing, though."

"What's that, little dove?" I rumble.

She wrinkles her nose in the cutest possible way. "I think maybe we both need a shower first."

Laughter rockets out of my throat. "You're right." I tried to clean up on the plane ride home, but I was covered in blood, and it's been a very long twenty-four hours since our last extremely pleasurable shower.

I scoop her back up and carry her to the bathroom. She laughs when I drop her to her feet and rip the stained and torn teal crop top off over her head. She works the buttons on my jeans as I tear her sports bra in half down the front.

"Darius!" she exclaims breathlessly. "How did you even do that? That should be impossible."

"Princess, there are at least a dozen things I'm going to do to you right now that you used to think were impossible."

"Oh yeah? Show me," she dares.

Challenge accepted.

I yank her yoga pants and panties down to her ankles, lowering to a squat as I do. When she kicks off the fabric from her ankles, I thread my arms between her legs, secure her back with my palms, and stand with her pussy at the level of my mouth. She shrieks, laughing and ducking, so her head doesn't hit the ceiling. I'm lost in her juicy essence. My tongue delves between her folds.

"Oh, God!" Her thighs clamp around my ears. "Darius." She wends her fingers into my rapidly-growing hair and pulls. "Oh, my God."

"I'll bet you didn't know this was possible," I taunt between rolls of my tongue.

Her cries fall like gold coins around me. Sparkling rewards just for doing what I was born to do. "Oh, please." She's quivering, her delicate flesh clenching and releasing. "It's...it's too much."

I know she only says that because she needs to come.

I spin to pin her hips against the wall, my hands shifting from behind her back to her armpits. Her legs dangle across my arms, feet kicking as I penetrate her with my tongue.

"Darius...Darius!" she sounds alarmed. "Oh my God, pleeeeease!" she screams, pulling my hair hard.

I suction my mouth over all of her sex, and she bucks against me in a release. She's sobbing with pleasure, shaking all over when I lower her gently to sit on the countertop while I turn on the water.

"Don't leave me," she murmurs, clinging to my arm as I turn away. "I don't think I can stay upright yet."

"I've got you, Princess." I steady her with a hand at her waist while I strip out of my jeans. I'm not wearing any boxers—my clothes shredded when I spontaneously shifted in the warehouse, but fortunately, the triplets brought spare clothes along when they rescued us.

The moment I'm naked, I test the water and, finding it warm, lift my beautiful mate into the stall with me. I let her stand under the warm spray of water while I take a bar of soap and roll it in my hands.

"Nope." Paloma reaches for it. "I want to wash you this time," she says, tugging me forward, so we change positions. "I need to feel these big strong bear muscles." Her hands find my waist and stroke up my sides, sliding in a slow circle around my pecs.

My dick is rock hard, straining toward her, pre-cum dripping from the head. Her obvious appreciation of my body makes me feel like my bear could rip out of me at any moment. Instead of shoving that sensation away, I lean into it. I don't let him out, but I meld with him. I allow my bear side into the moment.

An animal-like rumble comes from my chest.

Paloma's gaze shoots up from her admiration of my abs to my face. I don't find any fear in her expression, though. Only wonder. She lifts her hands to my face and strokes along my jaw then tugs my beard. "Your bear-eyes are showing."

I reach for her, the moment of letting her take control ending with a surge of lust. I grasp her ass and pull her body up against mine, lowering my head to take her mouth again. She wraps her fist around my cock, and I groan.

"Let me wash you," she murmurs against my mouth.

I marshal my control. "Your wish is my command, princess." I reluctantly release her, and she runs the bar of soap across my chest, under my armpits, then down my thighs, ignoring my extremely obvious erection.

"Turn around." Her voice is husky. Her nipples are taut.

I turn, and she soaps my back then circles her sudsy hands around my ass and between my cheeks, teasing my balls from behind.

"Ffffuuuck," I groan.

I can't wait any longer. I turn back around, but before I can take control, she fists my cock and holds me still. I nearly die when she slides her soapy palm up and down my shaft.

"Oh, sweet dove. You're going to make me come like a teenager. Hold off." I grasp her wrist, and she releases me.

I pick her up by the waist to change our places again and wash her, worshiping her with my hands at the same time my mouth roams her peaks and valleys, sucking, licking, nibbling everywhere that makes her scream.

"Okay!" she finally cries.

"Okay, what, sweet dove?"

"Okay, I think we're clean enough."

I laugh. "My bear agrees." I pick her up, turning the water off with my knee and carrying her out of the shower. I find a towel to wrap her in, but it doesn't stay on because thirty seconds later, I have her turned around, braced against the wall.

"Give me that ass," I rumble, kicking her legs wider.

She folds at the waist, offering herself up to me.

I mean to be far more suave. I meant for this to be a slow seduction, but it's too late. My bear is running the show, and he wants her *now*.

I rub the head of my throbbing cock along her slit, parting her sweet folds. I barely manage to hold back, remembering she's practically still a virgin. Her body isn't accustomed to my size. Squeezing my eyes closed tight to concentrate, to slow myself down, I feed my length into her, centimeter by centimeter.

She lets out wanton sounds. More gold coins falling around my ears.

"Let me into that tight, juicy pussy of yours." My voice sounds two octaves deeper than normal.

"You're in, you're in," she pants, pushing back against me, hollowing her lower back to take me deeper.

"Mmm, that's it, baby." I sink a little deeper. "So good. You take me so good. Oh, you like the dirty talk, don't you?" I croon when she grows even slicker, allowing me to get in even farther. I ease back an inch and slowly push forward again. "Hmm? You want me to fuck you hard from behind, princess? Is that what your Viking does?"

"My bear," she whimpers.

I stay where I am and reach around to gently tap her clit. She pushes back, taking more of my cock. "You want your bear?"

"Yes. Yes, please."

I stroke my hands along her sides, sliding around to mold them over her breasts and pinch her nipples, then back down to circle my thumbs around her lower back. "Mmm, you're asking me so nicely. I think I'd better give you a thorough fucking. What do you think?" I ease back further this time before I drop in deeper, bottoming out against her cervix.

She cries out.

"You need a good fucking, sweet dove?" I grip her waist and ease back, then plunge in with more force this time. She's dripping wet, soaking my cock with her juices, her flesh silky and plump and welcoming.

"Y-yes," she warbles.

I tighten my grip and quicken my pace, arcing in and out of her. I bite my cheek bloody to rein in my aggression. To keep from getting too rough with my beautiful mate.

"Is that good, princess? You like to take me deep?" I tap her clit again.

"God, yes," she breathes.

"Take it, then." I fuck her harder, my breath dragging in rough gusts across my teeth.

"Yes!" she cries. "I need you. I need you. I need you."

Her moans undo me. I lose control and pound into her, my fingers gripping too hard, my hips slapping into her gorgeous, cushioned ass.

The room spins. It's too hot–the steam from our shower still fogs up the mirror. I feel my canines descend, ready to mark my Paloma.

"Are you sure?" I rasp, somehow remembering again to get consent.

"Yes! I want this!" she cries.

I wrap my arm around her waist and grasp the front of her throat, lifting her away from the wall, so her head falls back against my shoulder as I thrust up into her. "Mine," I growl, my voice not sounding human at all. I rub her clit as I come, and she orgasms at the same moment I do. My teeth sink into the meaty part of her shoulder, forever embedding the serum coating my teeth into her flesh.

She jolts with the pain of it, and for one horrible moment, I think my bear is going to rampage, but I realize I have full control. I immediately retract my teeth from her flesh, licking away the blood and kissing up her neck. "That's it, sweet dove. It's over now," I murmur, my fingertip still stroking her clit. "You're mine now. My mate. Forever."

She orgasms again, trembling and gasping in my arms, her muscles clenching around my cock, milking another climax from me.

"I love you, Paloma. I love you so damn much. More than anyone or anything in my life."

Chapter Sixteen

Darius

She lets out a sob–whether it's emotional or a physical release, I can't be sure.

"Are you okay, sweetheart?" I hold her tight, continuing to kiss her everywhere my lips can reach. "I'm sorry I hurt you. I never want to hurt you again. Never."

"I know, it's okay. I'm okay." She sounds teary, so I pull out and swing her up into my arms to carry her to bed.

I'm relieved once I can see her face. She doesn't appear to be in pain–she looks like she's in ecstasy. My incredible, beautiful mate.

"Do you believe I love you?" I ask. "I want you to know–it's not just the pheromones. You *are* my fated mate, but it's so much more for me. I think you're incredible, Paloma. You're braver than any warrior and smart as hell. And you're kind and loyal. The sacrifices you made for your sister are–" My eyes get hot thinking of how I abandoned my brothers and Bad Bear Mountain while I told myself I was doing it all for them.

Paloma reaches for my face as I settle us onto the bed facing each other. "Are you thinking about Teddy?"

"I was thinking about all my brothers. What a fool I've been. I told myself I had to leave and build a fortune to save them all, but all I was doing was running from my bear."

"The bear that I love." She strokes my bearded jaw.

"You love my bear?" I'm fishing for her approval. Fate, it's shocking how vulnerable I feel right now. Paloma might not love me. She doesn't have bear pheromones to tell her I'm the male for her. But she did allow me to mark her. That must mean something.

"I love *you*," she says firmly, lifting her soft lips to press against mine. "*And* your bear. Because you are one and the same."

"You saved me," I realize. "I was half a male, with a completely unexpressed side I was in denial about. And you set me free. All this time, I thought I was saving you, but I had it backward. Just like I told myself I was saving my brothers by moving to New York."

"No," Paloma laughs, but there's a haunted quality to her expression. "You definitely saved me. God, I was literally enslaved. If you hadn't come along, I would be some asshole's sex slave in addition to Thom's stock trader slave right now." She shudders.

My bear surfaces with rage, and I let him growl out loud.

Paloma is unafraid. Her eyes crinkle as she presses another kiss to my lips. "There he is," she purrs.

We both sober, remembering what she's been through. "I can't believe Thom knew about shifters and wanted to hunt them."

I frown. "Yes, there's a secret society of ultra-wealthy

around the world who traffic shifters–more often juveniles about to transition. They call themselves Venatores."

"Right. Latin for *hunter.* Thom told me when you were passed out."

"Yes. They named themselves after the trained hunters in ancient Rome who participated in public spectacles called *venationes.* These spectacles involved hunting and killing wild animals in arenas and were a major form of entertainment. I guess to these modern-day Venatores, a shifter–a human wild animal–is a better opponent."

"Disgusting." Rage flares in Paloma's gaze, fierce and protective. "Those men are twisted. Morally reprehensible. They need to be brought down."

"Yes. That's the focus of the shifter ops team you met."

"And for fuck's sake, hunting *juveniles who just transitioned?* That's just sick."

"I agree."

"Maybe I can help. I know many of Thom's cronies."

"That would be helpful. I'm sure they will thoroughly investigate all leads you can provide or that they can dig up now that they know Thom was a part of it."

Paloma blinks at me, her gaze clouding even more. "Am I going to be wanted for murder now?"

"No." I tuck a section of hair behind her ear. "Absolutely not. The ops team stayed to clean up. I imagine they staged an explosion or a plane crash or something to cover it all up."

"Oh!" Paloma laughs. "I just realized that's why they lit off fireworks when we landed at Lockepoint. It was to cover the sound of gunfire! So smart."

"Yes." I lightly trace around wounds I made in Paloma's neck. "How much do you hate me right now for this?"

She laughs. "I might hate you tomorrow, but right now, I feel incredible."

I relax a little. "The serum may have some drugging properties to humans–I'm not sure. I'll ask Matthias. We should have him keep an eye on those puncture wounds to make sure they don't get infected although my saliva speeds healing and prevents infection."

"Okay." Paloma's lids droop, and her head falls into the pillow.

I believe we've both been up for twenty-four hours straight, except for when I was drugged, but it feels like there's so much we still need to discuss. "There's something I didn't tell you."

Paloma leans her head up on one hand, looking sleepy. "What is it?"

"Bears mate for life. Marking you is more than a human marriage. There's no divorcing me. No getting rid of me. But I don't want you to feel caged in after everything you've been through."

Paloma gazes at me with those big brown eyes. "Are you saying I'm stuck with you now?"

I nod.

"I'm going to have a giant, growly bear protector for the rest of my life?"

"That's right, princess. We don't have to stay here, though. I'll go wherever you and Wren want to live. I can work from anywhere, despite what I told myself for the last fifteen years."

"And he comes with seven giant bear brothers and a mom who is hibernating?"

I see the twinkle in her eye, and I'm able to exhale. "Exactly."

"Oh, darn." Her lips quirk, and she leans forward to kiss

my lips. "That sounds perfectly horrible, but I'll probably adjust."

I stroke my hand over her hip. "Are you sure, love? I know we just met, and humans normally court for much longer."

"I've never been so sure of anything in my life," she murmurs, scooting her pillow closer and nestling right up against my chest. "But now I need to hibernate for a minute," she mumbles sleepily.

My bear rumbles softly, content at last. My mate is here in my arms, exactly where she's supposed to be. I may have kidnapped Rapunzel from her tower, but now she's content to stay.

I press a reverent kiss to her forehead. "Sleep, little dove," I murmur, even though her breath is already deep and even.

* * *

Paloma

"Wake up."

"One thing you should know," I mumble. "I am not really a morning person." Years of Thom making me work early and overtime trading hours had me longing to sleep in.

"Good to know." Darius kisses my shoulder. He cut his hair back to Wall Street standards, which is sexy as hell. Actually, he rocks every length of hair and beard I've seen on him.

"Sleep all you want, princess. Just so you know, I've gotten word that Teddy and Lana invited us over for a big pancake breakfast."

My eyes pop open. "Never mind, I'm awake. I love pancakes."

Darius' chest rumbles with a laugh. "Wren told them they were your favorite. She and Everest made a Bananas Foster sauce on the side."

"I'm up, I'm up." I throw off the covers and dash to the bathroom.

"Take your time. I'll get you some coffee."

I exit the bedroom a few minutes later, all dressed in comfy GoddessWear yoga pants and a spaghetti strap top, with one of Darius' flannel shirts thrown over it for warmth. Darius greets me with a hot mug of coffee and a kiss.

"Mmmm, I could get used to this." I rub his stubbled chin. He was clean-shaven a minute ago, but now his jaw is covered in wiry golden hairs. "Viking beard kisses are the best."

"It's my bear," Darius mutters. "He's making his presence known."

"Hello, bear. Thanks again for saving our skin."

Darius leans down and lets his head fall. We stand forehead to forehead, communing for a moment. We've been through so much the past few days. So much adventure, and we survived. It's still sinking in that we're together and safe.

Something whinnies and snorts outside our door. It's a familiar sound–like a horses' chuff.

"What's that?" I crane my head.

"That is my brothers' welcome gift to you." He nudges me to the door. "They got some friends of ours to smuggle her out of Lockepoint."

I set down my coffee on a side table and step outside. Waiting in the clearing in front of the cabin is my horse, Starlight. "Oh, baby, here you are." I take her halter and kiss her nose. She nickers softly, greeting me.

Darius steps out, and she tosses her head, snorting and shying away.

206

"Shhhh, it's okay." I stroke her sides and let her back away from Darius.

"She smells my bear." He keeps his distance.

"She'll get used to you. I didn't like you at first, either." I make a face at him, and he grins.

Axel and the triplets stand at the edge of the woods. I lead Starlight over to them. Her ears prick but she lets me walk right up to them.

"Thank you all so much." I pull each of them into a hug. They have to bend down to reach me, but they might as well get used to doing it. I'm not going to grow any taller, and I have a feeling we'll be hugging a lot.

We're family now.

"She looks good. Who brushed her?"

The triplets all point at Axel.

"She doesn't mind me so much," he says and proves it by taking her halter and running his hands down her mane. "I cleaned out my other garage to make a stable for her."

"We can build a stable here," Darius offers.

"Does that mean..." Bern says, and Canyon finishes his sentence, "are you staying?"

I raise my brows at Darius.

"Up to you." He reaches for my hand. "If you're willing, I'm ready to come home."

I smile. "I'm willing. I'm more than willing. This place felt like home to me the moment I got here."

"Whooohooo," Hutch whoops, and when Starlight steps nervously, we all shush him.

"Yay," the other two triplets whisper. One of them uses the smallest possible motion to pump his fist in the air.

We walk up to Lana and Teddy's incredible Architecture Digest-worthy cabin, complete with an entire wall of windows that looks out into the woods.

Wren comes to the porch to give me another strangle-hug. "Pancake-time!"

She looks fresh and happy and alive–so different from the way she looked at Thom's or at boarding school. It's like something in her woke up when Thom died. Or maybe it was when she got here. It's hard to believe she's so comfortable when she just spent the last couple of days and nights with complete strangers.

"Sorry I slept so long. Have you been okay up here?" The big sister in me still needs to tend to her, even though she's clearly thriving.

"We love having her!" Lana arrives from the kitchen and gives me a welcoming hug.

"Yes, I love it here," Wren says. "I think we should stay."

I laugh and glance up at Darius, who continues to flank me, taking his job as my guardian bear-mate all too seriously. "That's exactly what we were thinking."

"Oh good!" She bounces on her feet. "Because I already told them you couldn't live here without Starlight, and they went and got her."

"You were responsible for that?" My face feels like it might split in two from smiling so big. It's almost hard to hold this much happiness.

To feel everything could be so perfect.

"Yep." Wren's gaze wanders to the door, like she's looking for one or all of the triplets.

At that moment, the door bangs open and Canyon, Bern, Hutch and Axel all spill in.

"Pancakes, pancakes, pancakes!" All three triplets chant. Even in Lana and Teddy's giant house, their presence fills the space.

"Settle down," Matthias commands. He's sitting on the

couch, reading a book. He doesn't even have to look up, and the triplets calm.

I notice Wren has an extra spark of energy when she sashays to the kitchen. "They're ready—come and sit down!"

Teddy emerges from the kitchen with a platter of pancakes heaped higher than his head. The triplets break into cheers.

Darius and I follow them to the giant dining room and take a seat. A moment later, a shadow falls over me. In the window looms a huge light brown bear.

Everest.

He's on hind legs with his paws resting on the window. His black nose smears the glass.

Teddy sets the pancakes down and motions to the bear. "Get down."

The bear angles his head to the side. Even though he's huge, his little round ears are adorable.

"Aww, he's hungry." Wren sets down a platter of different flavored syrups and a saucepot of the bananas foster topping she made because it's my favorite. She drops into a seat beside me.

"You can't come in," Teddy lectures Everest. "No bear forms in the house."

"Everest," Matthias states quietly.

Everest drops out of sight. I'm not sure when I'm going to get used to seeing a giant bear just hanging out inside a house. Or on a rugby field.

"Will I ever meet him in human form?" I murmur.

Darius stretches his arm over the back of my chair. "He's shy. We're opposites. I never let my bear out. He stays in bear form all the time."

"He needs to get used to being a man," Teddy says with

an unhappy look at Matthias who's seated at the head of the table.

Matthias nods. "We're working on it."

"We're trying to set the 'no bear forms in the house' rule now before the baby comes," Lana whispers to us. She rubs her round belly, biting her lip. She looks a little guilty, watching Everest lumber off into the woods.

"Good rule," Darius says, stacking pancakes onto my and Wren's plates. "It would've kept Teddy and me from destroying our bunk beds three times."

"Us too," Hutch says around a mouthful of food.

Axel elbows him. "Don't talk with your mouth full."

"Remember that one Christmas—" Bern starts, and Canyon laughs, interrupting to say, "We thought we'd catch Santa coming down the chimney—"

"And we tore apart the mortar holding the stones," Hutch ends the story. The triplets and Axel crack up with laughter. Even Matthias chuckles.

Hutch sobers. "It destroyed the structural integrity of the cabin, and we had to move."

"Yeah, good times," Canyon says, and the other triplets elbow him.

Teddy rubs a hand over his face. "No wonder our mother is hibernating."

I sneak a glance at Darius, but he's smiling, his face clear. He's no longer triggered by the stories of him and his brother's out-of-control bears.

After breakfast, Darius and I go on a hike. Wren and triplets troop along behind us, carrying picnic baskets full of pancakes. After a few minutes, they split off to find Everest.

Darius and I wander hand in hand on a worn trail. The forest is peaceful, with birds chirping and fluttering from tree to tree. There's a smoky edge to the chilly air. Winter is coming. Thanksgiving is almost here.

I have a lot to be thankful for. My family is safe. Wren, Starlight, and I will have the freedom we've always longed for, plus all the love and support of our newfound family. This morning's breakfast was a taste of the gentle chaos of being around so many boisterous bears, and I soaked it in. Wren did too. She's already made herself at home.

Plus, it's nice to know, if anyone threatens us, the bears could make mincemeat of our enemies.

"So you're good with this?" Darius breaks the silence. "Staying on Bad Bear Mountain?"

"I was just thinking this place is paradise. Fresh air, gorgeous views. A sexy Viking in my bed." I tilt my head. "What about you? Will you miss New York?"

He blows out a breath. I think part of him is coming to terms with how much he loves his family and his home. How much he belongs here. "Not really. My employees mostly work remotely. I could let the lease on my office and penthouse go tomorrow. I wouldn't even have stuff to pack."

"It was never really your home," I say.

"No."

I keep silent for a few paces, letting that sink in. "There's nothing to keep us from visiting."

"Yeah, I'd like that. I do have some friends I'd like you to meet. Sully, the guy who helped us get to the safe house, is one of them. But I think the mountain is where we belong."

I smile, but then have a thought. "What about Lockepoint?"

"I have people looking into it. Thom's estate is tied up with creditors. And from what Kylie can tell from her hacking, a lot of his wealth was gifted to a few private companies dedicated to conservation."

"Like...conservation efforts to save the earth?"

His expression turns grim. "We think they might really be shell corporations for the Venatores."

A chill runs through me. The Venatores are still out there. Still a threat.

"You and Wren are safe here," Darius says.

"I know. Thank you." This is probably the safest place in the world for us.

"We'll keep digging. But when it comes to Lockepoint... I don't know if you and Wren will get any inheritance."

I shrug. "That's okay. We don't need his blood money. I can make my own." I squeeze his hand. "I'm still waiting for an official invite to work at Mountain Top Investments."

Darius goes still. "You'd do that? Come work with me?"

I face him. "Of course. I like trading. I just don't want to be anyone's slave."

"Then consider this your official offer. How's fifty percent ownership sound?"

"Perfect." I let him take me into his arms and dip me for a kiss.

"I love you, little dove," he murmurs just before he claims my mouth.

"I love you, my Viking bear." I kiss him back.

* * *

Don't worry, it's not quite over! Read on for a special epilogue about Lana's baby shower, starring Lana, Paloma, Wren, plus some out of town guests from Taos. And, of course, the Bad Boy Bears.

Epilogue

Paloma

The day of Lana's baby shower is a gorgeous, crisp fall day. Darius and I hike up early to help, but Lana hired a whole party planning team, so when we arrive there's a full buffet brunch laid out on the dining table and a big tent with tables already set up outside.

There's a rainbow colored balloon arch and tablecloths patterned with rainbows being clutched at either end by little brown bears.

"Not pink and baby blue?" I tease Lana. She's in a periwinkle blue lounge set with a few matching blue braids scattered in with her soft pink ones.

"I wanted all the colors. Teddy wanted brown, for his bear, so the brown bears are for him."

The party planners have all disappeared, but I still lower my voice. "Do you think the baby will be a shifter?"

"Teddy says probably," Lana says, and Teddy appears as if summoned. He strides to his mate's side and leans down to plant a kiss on the top of her head.

"I bet our children will all be bears."

"Brown bears?" I ask. "Like you and Darius?"

"Yes." Teddy couldn't puff out his chest more if he tried.

"Although Everest is hoping that the baby will have a bear that's a cross between a grizzly and a polar bear like him."

"Is that genetically possible?"

"No," Lana and Teddy say in unison.

"Are you going to explain that to Everest?"

Teddy just sighs.

Everest's bear form moves around the tables. I'm guessing Lana made sure the party would be outside, so he could come.

I mention this to Darius, and he nods. "We're having a family meeting soon to talk to him about shifting back into human form. I think he's been living off the land like a bear."

I want to ask him more, but Lana's guests arrive. She had a big party in LA for her celebrity friends to attend, so this one is for shifter friends and family.

Standing beside Darius, it's almost too much to take in—there's so much love. So much togetherness. After ten years of solitude, I suddenly have everything. It feels like my heart will burst.

Hutch and Bern helicoptered in women from Taos. They're the human mates of Rafe, Lance, and Deke, the guys who helped rescue Wren. Adele, Charlie, and Sadie are all close with Lana.

"Are the guys coming?" Lana asks, giving each woman a hug.

"They're on babysitting duty," Charlie says. "Girls' trip only, and we didn't drive, so we can drink!"

I offer her a spiked cider, and she thanks me with a sigh.

"They do send their congratulations," Sadie says. "And

Deke and Lance fought over which one would give you a baby carrier as a gift. They have strong opinions on baby carriers."

"How are your twins, Sadie?" Lana asks.

"Keeping us up all hours," Sadie says with a tired smile. "Ansel is a night owl, and Bonnie wakes up at the crack of dawn. Luckily, Deke functions fine on low sleep."

"You want some coffee?" Wren offers her.

"Or spiked cider?" I hold up my tray.

"How about some spiked coffee." Sadie says.

"Now you're talking." Adele lights up, and we all laugh.

After our boozy brunch, we do gifts. Adele owns a chocolate shop in Taos. She brought gifts for all of us, golden and white boxes with little chocolate bears. Lana loves the books we bought for the nursery. Teddy and Darius both model different sorts of baby carriers, using two teddy bears as baby models.

My ovaries really like seeing Darius holding a 'baby.' He catches me staring at him, and his eyes light up gold. I look away before his bear gets ideas.

Wren leans into me. "Are you and Darius gonna make me an aunt?"

I playfully swat her arm. "Not for a while yet. We want a little time to ourselves. And I want to build my career."

"I'm just saying, Darius would be a great stay-at-home dad."

I shush her. Werebears have super sensitive hearing. "Don't tempt me." When I look up again, he's got a sexy smolder directed my way, and I decide if he puts a baby bear in me sooner rather than later, I won't mind.

"Are you going to do a gender reveal?" Charlie asks Lana.

"It's too early. Besides, Bern spent three hours yesterday

explaining that there's more than just a gender binary." Lana smiles up at the goth triplet. He clears his throat as if he's about to launch into the explanation, and Hutch and Canyon grab him and clap a hand over his mouth.

"I did ask the doctor to give us some pictures of the last ultrasound," Lana says. "We haven't seen them yet." She holds up an envelope. "Teddy, will you do the honors?"

He takes the envelope and lets an accordion of black and white images unfold almost to the floor. It takes a few seconds for us to parse what we're seeing.

"Baby one," Lana reads the label on the top image. There's a set of images and then another label. "Baby two."

Teddy's hand starts shaking. Lana grabs the lowest set of pictures. We all stare at the third label.

"Baby three," Darius reads.

Teddy's eyes are wide, and his lips are frozen. Darius takes the pictures and lays them out on the table. Lana leans in, her hands on her stomach.

"Does this mean...?"

"It means," Matthias says, with impeccable bedside manner, "you're having triplets."

There's a stunned pause.

"Yeeeah," the triplets whoop. Axel starts slow clapping.

Sadie has her hands over her face, laughing helplessly.

"Congratulations, brother." Matthias claps Teddy on the back. Teddy staggers a little, and Axel steadies him.

"Don't worry." Darius steps in to hug his twin. "We'll all babysit."

"Yeah!" agree the triplets.

Teddy looks like he's about to pass out. "I don't know whether to thank you or to tell you to stay the hell away from my kids."

"Come here." Lana waves to him, and he goes to her.

He sinks down to his knees in front of her armchair and lets his forehead fall against hers. We all look away to give them a private moment.

"It's okay, Papa Bear," Lana murmurs. "We got this."

"I love you, babygirl." Teddy's voice is all choked up.

After an extended minute of kissing, Matthias clears his throat. "Come on, brother. Let's get a drink. And then maybe all of us uncles can practice putting on diapers." He and Darius lead a shell-shocked Teddy away.

Lana claps her hands. "Who wants a tour of the nursery?"

"I take it back," I whisper to Wren as we follow Lana inside. "If twins and triplets run in the family, I might just keep my legs closed."

"Good luck with that," Wren cackles.

It's afternoon before we wrap up the party with the final activity.

"The brothers had a pumpkin pie baking contest," Lana announces. "The winner gets to make the pies for Thanksgiving. Adele, will you judge?"

"Of course." She leads the way back outside to a table decorated with pumpkins to showcase eight pumpkin pies.

Matthias jogs up the path toward the tables, a wide smile on his face. "Brothers—and sisters—gather up. Come here, all of you."

I get to Darius, and he loops an arm around my shoulders and pulls me close. Together, we walk toward Matthias.

The triplets ignore him until he puts his fingers to his lips and whistles, and then they all jerk their heads up to look. He beckons to them.

Axel, Everest, and the triplets all join Darius, Teddy, Lana, and me around Matthias.

"I have some news," Matthias says, his voice strong but gentle. "I just came from Mom's cabin."

"Mom?" Teddy asks.

"Yes," Matthias says. "That's what I'm here to tell everyone. Mom's awake."

* * *

We hope you've enjoyed Alpha's Claim *and Darius and Paloma's story. If you did, we would so appreciate your review. They make a huge difference to indie authors.*

If you haven't read Teddy and Lana's book (Alpha's Rescue) *yet, click here.*

For Jackson and Kylie's book (Alpha's Temptation), *click here.*

And don't miss all the Taos couples in our Shifter Ops series!

Love and growly bear brothers,

Renee & Lee

Click here to read a BONUS short holiday story: A Bad Bear Thanksgiving

https://geni.us/badboybearthanksgiving

Want FREE books?

Want FREE books?

220

Other Titles by Renee Rose

Paranormal

Werewolves of Wall Street

Big Bad Boss: Midnight

Big Bad Boss: Moon Mad

Big Bad Boss: Marked

Big Bad Boss: Mated

Wolf Ridge High Series

Alpha Bully

Alpha Knight

Step Alpha

Alpha King

Alpha Varsity

Bad Boy Alphas Series

Alpha's Temptation

Alpha's Danger

Alpha's Prize

Alpha's Challenge

Alpha's Obsession

Alpha's Desire

Alpha's War

Alpha's Mission

Alpha's Bane

Alpha's Secret

Alpha's Prey

Alpha's Sun

Shifter Ops

Alpha's Moon

Alpha's Vow

Alpha's Revenge

Alpha's Fire

Alpha's Rescue

Alpha's Command

Bad Boy Bears

Alpha's Claim

Alpha Doms Series

The Alpha's Hunger

The Alpha's Promise

The Alpha's Punishment

The Alpha's Protection (Dirty Daddies)

Two Marks Series

Untamed

Tempted

Desired

Enticed

Wolf Ranch Series

Rough

Alpha Mountain

Hero

Rebel

Warrior

Vegas Underground Mafia Romance

King of Diamonds

Mafia Daddy

Jack of Spades

Ace of Hearts

Joker's Wild

His Queen of Clubs

Dead Man's Hand

Wild Card

Daddy Rules Series

Fire Daddy

Hollywood Daddy

Stepbrother Daddy

Master Me Series

Her Royal Master

Her Russian Master

Her Marine Master

Yes, Doctor

Double Doms Series

Theirs to Punish

Theirs to Protect

Holiday Feel-Good

Scoring with Santa

Saved

Other Contemporary

Black Light: Valentine Roulette

Black Light: Roulette Redux

Black Light: Celebrity Roulette

Black Light: Roulette War

Black Light: Roulette Rematch

Punishing Portia (written as Darling Adams)

The Professor's Girl

Safe in his Arms

Sci-Fi

Zandian Masters Series

His Human Slave

His Human Prisoner

Training His Human

His Human Rebel

His Human Vessel

His Mate and Master

Zandian Pet

Their Zandian Mate

His Human Possession

Zandian Brides

Night of the Zandians

Also by Lee Savino

Paranormal romance

<u>The Berserker Saga</u> and <u>Berserker Brides</u> (menage werewolves)

These fierce warriors will stop at nothing to claim their mates.

<u>Draekons (Dragons in Exile) with Lili Zander</u> (menage alien dragons)

Crashed spaceship. Prison planet. Two big, hulking, bronzed aliens who turn into dragons. The best part? The dragons insist I'm their mate.

<u>Bad Boy Alphas with Renee Rose (bad boy werewolves)</u>

Never ever date a werewolf.

<u>Tsenturion Masters with Golden Angel</u>

Who knew my e-reader was a portal to another galaxy? Now I'm stuck with a fierce alien commander who wants to claim me as his own.

Contemporary Romance

<u>Royal Bad Boy</u>

I'm not falling in love with my arrogant, annoying, sex god boss. Nope. No way.

<u>Royally Fake Fiancé</u>

The Duke of New Arcadia has an image problem only a fiancé can fix. And I'm the lucky lady he's chosen to play Cinderella.

<u>Beauty & The Lumberjacks</u>

After this logging season, I'm giving up sex. For...reasons.

About Renee Rose

USA TODAY BESTSELLING AUTHOR RENEE ROSE loves a dominant, dirty-talking alpha hero! She's sold over two million copies of steamy romance with varying levels of kink. Her books have been featured in USA Today's *Happily Ever After* and *Popsugar*. Named Eroticon USA's Next Top Erotic Author in 2013, she has also won *Spunky and Sassy's* Favorite Sci-Fi and Anthology author, *The Romance Reviews* Best Historical Romance, and has hit the *USA Today* list fifteen times with her Bad Boy Alphas, Chicago Bratva, and Wolf Ranch series.

Renee loves to connect with readers!
www.reneeroseromance.com
reneeroseauthor@gmail.com

f facebook.com/reneeroseromance

instagram.com/reneeroseromance

BB bookbub.com/authors/renee-rose

goodreads.com/ReneeRose

About Lee Savino

Lee Savino is a USA today bestselling author, mom and chocoholic.

Warning: Do not read her Berserker series, or you will be addicted to the huge, dominant warriors who will stop at nothing to claim their mates.

I repeat: Do. Not. Read. The Berserker Saga.

Download a free book from www.leesavino.com (don't read that either. Too much hot, sexy lovin').